THE ART OF

Loving

KRISTI COPELAND

TEXAS
SUMMER
NIGHTS

THE ART OF Loving

KRISTI COPELAND

Twisted Tales Publishing 2022

The Art of Loving

Copyright © 2022 Kristi Copeland

Twisted Tales Publishing 2022

This book is a work of fiction. Names, characters, businesses, organiza- tions, places, events and incidents either are the product of the author's imagination or are used fictitiously. Any resemblance to actual persons, living or dead, events, or locales is entirely coincidental.

For information contact :

https://kristicopelandwriter.com/

Cover design: Pretty Indie: Book Cover Designs

Editor: Kerri Boehm

Formatting Template : Derek Murphy

ISBN: 978-1-7376339-7-6 (paperback) 978-1-7376339-6-9 (ebook)

Also by Kristi Copeland

TEXAS SUMMER NIGHTS

Somewhere Outside of Sunset - Book 1

Home in Paradise - Book 2

OTHER WORKS

Oakdale

COMING SOON

Heaven Scent

Scan the QR Code to be directed to Kristi's author page:

SCAN ME

For my husband:

My love, my king, my everything.

CONTENTS

The Chicken Coop

Saturday, August 12, 2017

"COME ON, CHICKIE, we do this every day. Why do you have to peck at me? You should be used to this by now." Jason Payne lifted his best laying hen with a spade shovel and reached under her warm feathers to grab three eggs. The hen pecked at the metal and clucked in response to her owner's voice.

Out of the corner of his eye, Jason caught a glimpse of something moving in the shadows. Chickie started to make more of a ruckus than usual in the dark hen house. A two-foot-long rat snake slithered across the rafters and dropped to eye-level before Jason had time to figure out what was happening.

A shriek loud enough to wake the dead escaped Jason's throat and he shuffled his feet as if trying to avoid stepping on a mouse. His hands shook and his spine tingled as he opened the door without a second thought. The gun he had brought with him every morning leaned against the wall. Hot metal met the palm of his hand.

The first blast left a large hole in the ceiling and Jason swore under his breath. He must have grabbed the rifle instead of a shotgun that morning. "Shit!" he said out loud before aiming at the slithering menace and firing again.

He knew there would be a mess to clean up, but he wasn't about to let that snake live. Not only would the reptile consume all the eggs, but those critters gave Jason the creeps.

Once the snake hit the floor and hissed, Jason took another shot but missed a third time. Feathers flew around his head as he tried to focus in the dark. Unharmed chickens clucked and carried on as background noise as he lifted the gun in the air. The snake finally stopped moving after three whacks with the butt of the gun.

The spade shovel served a dual purpose that day; first, lifting Chickie for eggs, then carrying a dead snake out of the hen house.

When the chickens were out of harm's way, Jason was able to talk himself out of the panic, although his heart continued to race. "Damn it, I need to install some lights in here." After he assessed the damage, he pursed his lips. "And, apparently, plug some holes." He ducked under the door and let it slam behind him.

Sunlight blinded Jason for a moment and he leaned against the side of the building. He closed his eyes, removed his cowboy hat, and ran a hand through his thick, dark, shaggy hair.

As his heartrate slowed and feeling returned to his legs, he turned in a slow circle to search for any human that may have witnessed the scene and said a silent prayer that the new neighbor had not heard the commotion.

Just my luck, Jason thought to himself as a lady with long, blonde hair pulled into a ponytail hollered from halfway across the yard.

"Hey! Are you okay?" Paint spattered her white tank top and a streak of blue underlined one eye. "I heard gunshots." The woman surveyed the yard and chicken coop. "Where's your little girl? Is she ok?" She pushed through the gate that separated their yards and rushed toward Jason.

Stunned by the lean but muscular tanned legs that stretched from flip-flops to short jean shorts, Jason couldn't remember what she had said just three seconds earlier.

"Sir, are you ok? Where's your little girl? I just heard a gunshot and a scream. Is she ok?"

Confused, Jason shook his head. "I don't have a little

girl." He squinted at the stranger and offered a bashful smile. "I don't think we've met. I'm Jason." He outstretched a hand in greeting.

"Wait." She took a step back. "Is everything ok? Seriously, I heard a girl scream." Her eyebrows knitted together as she turned toward him. "What's going on?" Standing with hands on hips, she meant business.

Jason looked at the ground and kicked the dirt with a dusty cowboy boot. "Yeah. No girl. That was me. I killed a snake." He raised his eyes to meet hers. "I hate snakes."

"You killed a snake. With a gun?" The woman laughed. "You shot a snake?"

"Yeah, but I missed. I really need to rethink which gun I want by my side next time I'm in the chicken coop." He glanced behind him at the small barn that housed his chickens.

The neighbor laughed. "How did you kill the snake if you didn't shoot it?"

As if to show her his success, Jason held up the firearm and nodded toward the butt of the gun. He pursed his lips instead of explaining.

The woman gasped and slapped her knee before letting out a loud laugh. "Wow, you really do hate snakes."

Shaking his head, Jason responded, "Yeah. I don't like 'em. Like, at all." One hand rested on his hip while he waited for her to stop giggling. He raised his eyebrows. "You done?" That made her start laughing all over again.

The tone of her voice and the way her eyes crinkled when she smiled made Jason grin and he couldn't help but chuckle at his own mishap. "Yeah, yeah, real funny," He held out his hand again. "Jason Payne."

The woman reached out to shake his hand, "Pam Waite. Nice to meet you."

"Pam," Jason repeated and smiled. *So, this gorgeous specimen is my new neighbor. Hot damn.* "You've been here for a couple weeks now?" When Pam tilted her head, Jason added, "I'm very observant. I like to know what's going on around my property."

"You're not a creeper, are you?" She took a step back and looked behind her as if she were about to run.

This time, Jason let out a loud laugh, "No, Pam. I'm not a creeper." Then he narrowed his eyes. "Do I look like a creeper?"

"Dude, you never know," Pam lifted both hands, palms out, and took another step back.

Jason nodded, "I'm just a simple rancher." Using his best nice-guy smile, he spread his arms wide and showed that he had nothing to hide. "What you see is what you get."

"A rancher that's afraid of snakes," Pam snickered. She shaded her eyes with one hand to get a better look at her fascinating neighbor.

Dark hair and dark eyes made his smile shine. "Funny."

Pam giggled.

"Listen, could I interest you in some tea or lemonade? Since we're neighbors and all."

"Tempting." Pam bit her lower lip and tilted her head. "Actually, I'm right in the middle of something." She watched Jason's expression fall. "Can I have a rain check?"

Emu Wrangling

Monday, August 14, 2017

MUSIC BLARED FROM the radio in Pam's shed-turned-painting studio. She blended a harsh pink acrylic paint into a muted orange on a fresh canvas. "There's something about Texas sunsets that can't be ignored."

Focused on Sam Hunt's voice and the beat of his number-one hit, "Body Like a Back Road," Pam's long blonde hair swished across her bare shoulders as she allowed the rhythm to consume her.

Dressed in a spaghetti-strap tank top and jean shorts, she tolerated the early morning heat. The air-conditioner blew lukewarm air into the small room as if on its last leg.

The song's description of a man taking his time to trace his girl's body made Pam think of her new neighbor. A fantasy of his lips on her skin repeated from the previous night and added to the warmth in the studio. She couldn't put a finger on exactly what it was about "Jason."

The sound of his name brought a smirk to her lips. She thoroughly enjoyed looking at him and wondered what it would feel like to kiss him, for his arms to wrap around her waist. Heat rose up her neck at the thought. Maybe it was his slow Texas drawl or how his cowboy hat sat low on his brow. It could be the way his jeans fit just right or the dimple in his left cheek.

A loud squawk broke Pam's concentration and she looked out the small window; to her surprise, three gigantic bird-like creatures were wandering around her backyard.

"What the—?"

One of the animals stood around seven feet tall with two smaller versions following the motions of the grazing adult. Pam had never seen an emu in person and thought they would be uglier.

She placed her brush in a tin can filled with water and opened the door to get a better look at the odd creatures. *I wonder if they're nice. Will they let me pet them? Can you pet a bird? How does that work?*

The adolescent birds must have sensed her presence and began to jog toward her studio while the larger emu wandered behind them. *That must be their mom.* She caught the motion of her neighbor in her peripheral and thanked the attraction gods for sending him her way.

Jason hurried through the gate that separated the

properties and left it open. "Come on, you feathered freaks," he called to the animals as if they understood. He caught a glimpse of Pam standing in the open doorway of the small shed and shook his head. He swore to himself as he tried to catch his breath; those shorts would certainly cause him to act a fool.

"Jason?"

The sound of his name on her lips caused him to stop short. Sexy thoughts of running his hands over her smooth skin entered his mind; he wondered if her kiss would set him on fire. "Oh, man. I'm in trouble," he whispered to himself.

His birds were loose and he had to secure them in their pasture before he allowed himself to think about touching Pam.

"Hey there." Jason lifted his chin and then his hand in a wave. "Ever wrangle an emu?"

With a tilt of her head, Pam squinted. "Have I ever what?"

"Wrangled an emu," Jason repeated. "I could really use your help getting these creatures back to their yard.

"Um…" Pam hesitated. "No. I can't honestly say that I've ever even seen an emu." Not one to shy away from a new adventure, she eyed the birds and tried to visualize capturing one of the babies. "What do I do? How do you catch these things?"

The studious look on her face made Jason chuckle. "You got to hug 'em, babe. Like this." With his arms stretched out to his sides, Jason bent at the waist and started to herd a small emu into one corner of the fence.

When he was close enough, he grabbed the bird from behind, wrapping his arms around the front of its chest, and straddled it. "Be careful not to hurt their arms. Wings. Whatever," he advised and shot a smile her way that made her wonder if what she had heard about Texas summer nights was true. Some said the nights were hotter here— in a good way.

She caught herself smirking and forced herself to focus. Following Jason's lead, Pam chased the other small emu. After she had it cornered, she reached out and grabbed it by the neck. "Please don't break. Please don't break," she said more to herself than to the bird. She moved her arms to circle the bird's chest as she stood over it like he had shown her.

Jason kept an eye on her to make sure she was okay. "That's it. You're doing great." The birds would be fine. This wasn't their first rodeo. Literally. It was a weekly occurrence for them to escape and for him to play emu cowboy.

Together, Jason and Pam guided the younger emus through the gate and into their home pasture. The older emu followed the youngsters into the enclosure and allowed the gate to be secured behind them.

Throughout the commotion, Pam dismissed the fact that Jason called her babe. Although she couldn't ignore how it made her cheeks warm, such a simple term of endearment usually didn't make her swoon. Even in her past relationships, when a guy called her 'honey' or 'baby' for the first time, she'd cringed. It never seemed natural. Until today.

Once they had safely captured the emus, Pam ran the back of her wrist across her forehead to push rogue blonde curls away from her green eyes.

Jason leaned against a fence post and chuckled; he captured her gaze and stared just a little too long. "It's not every day that you get to wrangle an emu."

"Right?" Pam exhaled and hoped he didn't notice her blush. "Lemonade?" she offered.

Jason nodded, lifted his cowboy hat, and ran one hand through his hair. The three-day scruff on his face and the dark hair that curled over his ears validated his father's most recent nickname for him: Shaggy. "That'd be great."

∩∩∩

CHIPPED PAINT AND two ginger cats covered the railing on Pam's back deck. She had filled two plastic cups with sweet pink liquid and handed one to Jason before automatically running her hand along both felines. "These guys yours or did the previous owner just abandon them?"

"I hope Boots and Woody aren't a bother. They've lived here for a really long time. Yes and no, to answer your question."

"No bother, they're sweet. I haven't ever had any pets, so it's nice to have them around. They're good listeners." Pam set her cup on the table between two rocking chairs before she lowered herself into one and nodded an invitation for Jason to sit to the other.

A slight breeze kept the Texas heat from forcing them inside. Pam's hair blew away from her face and she fanned her tank top, forcing spurts of rose scent toward Jason.

"Mmm, just the right amount of sugar." He sipped the cool drink. "Not too sweet." He took another sip, leaned back in the rocker, and sighed. "Thanks for your help with Alice and the twins."

"Alice?" Pam giggled. "You named your emu Alice? What are the twins' names? Tweedledee and Tweedledum?"

A frown shifted Jason's expression. "Too obvious?"

Pam threw her head back and laughed in response.

The sound echoed in his mind and was every bit as enjoyable as listening to his favorite song. He tried to ignore the pace of his heartbeat but failed. "Yeah, I guess so." A slow grin spread across his lips.

"I have a confession," he admitted, changing the subject. "I've been looking for a reason to see you again. These stupid emus escape regularly; should have known it would be Alice that brought me here."

Pam's eyebrows lifted as she waited for an explanation. She took a sip of the lemonade and rocked.

Jason licked his lips, glanced at his boots, then met her eyes, "I've been wondering..." He hesitated.

"Wondering what?" Curious, Pam tilted her head.

"Well, I haven't seen any other vehicles in your driveway, so I wondered..." A slow blink, then a lift of his shoulders filled a pause. "Is there a Mr. Pam?"

That's not what I expected. Not sure if she wanted to go down the road of drudging up semi-fresh wounds, Pam hesitated, then stood and excused herself.

"Open mouth, insert foot," Jason said to the cats. "Damn, you sure know how to be smooth, Shaggy." Mentally kicking himself, he shook his head and exhaled.

Pam returned and offered a soft smile. A bottle of rum, and two shot glasses filled her hands. "It's five-o-clock somewhere, right?" After pouring a shot into each of their glasses, she sat in the rocker and began to tell her story.

"It's only been a few months, so I'm still a little

bitter." She rolled her eyes, which made Jason smile. "I honestly don't know why I'm bitter. I should have known; the red flags were there from day one." She raised her glass as an invitation to not drink alone. Jason joined her in the salute, then waited for an explanation.

The shot went down smoother than she anticipated and she found herself wanting another.

Jason raised his eyebrows, interested in what she had to say.

After a sigh, Pam pursed her lips, looked away, and began to speak. "I was engaged when I moved here. My ex's family thrived on chaos and made everything overly dramatic, which forced him to escape through substances. I was fine with him drinking, but when that got excessive and he started using drugs to self-medicate, I drew the line."

Jason listened as a friend; he had been surprised by how comfortable he had quickly become sitting next to Pam. He pushed aside the thoughts of what it would be like to kiss her and focused on her words as she opened her heart.

"I could never understand what part of his life was so bad that he chose to take drugs. I mean, his family was rich. Filthy," She turned her gaze to Jason and raised her eyebrows for emphasis. "I gave him an ultimatum, and he chose crack and meth over me."

"I'm sorry, Pam." Jason exhaled.

An emotionless shrug told Jason that she had gotten over her ex before she physically broke it off. "Besides, I was too wild and crazy for him." She lifted one eyebrow and Jason's eyes widened. "I like to make a statement. I'm not afraid to show my true self. I like adventure, love to travel, and my bucket list is full of off-the-wall ideas that I wholly intend to carry out before I die. I'm not for everyone. I just haven't found anyone that is one-hundred-percent compatible with me; I'm not willing to settle."

"Good for you. No one should settle. So, were you engaged when you made the offer on this house or..." Not wanting to make any assumptions, he let his sentence trail off.

"No. I moved to Dallas last year. It took me over six months to figure out what was going on and what to do about it. I love Texas and didn't see any reason to go back to Colorado."

Pam found her glass empty and poured more rum into it. Jason smiled and followed her lead. "So, here I am. What about you, cowboy. What's your story?"

Although it was obvious she hadn't shared every detail with him, she did share a portion of her past. Jason thought it only respectful to do the same. For now, they both left open spaces.

"Well, my life hasn't been very exciting. I was born

and raised here in Loving and followed in the family business of raising cattle. I've made some changes and added bison to the herd a couple years ago." His eyes searched the neighboring pastures as he spoke.

"I asked my high school sweetheart to marry me when we were twenty. The wedding was planned for this time last year. Found out she cheated on me with a rodeo star. They ran away together a week before we were to be married. Then, just like a country song, my best friend died. A chocolate lab I got from my mom on my fourteenth birthday. I still miss Rocky every day."

A gasp brought his attention back to Pam. Her hand was covering her mouth. "I'm so sorry. That's just awful."

"Yeah. Thanks. It was for the best. She wanted to be with someone more exciting. Obviously, that wasn't me. Honestly, though, losing Rocky hurt more. I still haven't been inspired enough to get another dog. Hurts too much when they leave."

During the extended pause that came next, Pam closed her eyes and enjoyed the sounds of summer. Crickets, cats, and cows created unique noises in every direction.

"Listen," Pam opened her eyes to find Jason watching her. Pleased, she smiled. "I've known you less than three days and I can truly say that you're the most exciting person I've met in the past year." She laughed at

Jason's confused expression and explained. "Um, you shot holes in your chicken coop trying to kill a snake and you taught me to wrestle emus like a champ."

"That's different; that's just normal everyday life," with a shrug, he met Pam's gaze. "I don't go looking for adventures or sign up for crazy activities. I don't travel much; I'm kind of a homebody. That's not to say I'm not intrigued or interested; I just never seem to find the time."

Pam took another swig of rum and passed the bottle to Jason. "What do you do with your time when you're not tending chickens, emus, and bison?"

"My first love is animals. I ride my horses, feed my cats, and hug my asses." Amused by Pam's wide eyes and gaping mouth, Jason elaborated. "I have a family of donkeys that I think are the funniest critters I've ever encountered."

"Oh? I've only ever seen donkeys on TV or videos. I would love to meet them."

The smile Pam shared with Jason made his mind foggy. The energy surrounding her lit her face as if a direct sunbeam shone on her. He nearly forgot what they were discussing. "Meet who?"

"The donkeys, silly."

"Oh. Yeah." Jason shook his head. "The donkeys. They call to me whenever they see me; the way they bray makes me smile every time I hear them." Changing the subject, he said, "You mentioned that you love to travel. I've never been east of the Mississippi or west of the Rockies. I've really ever only travelled to Oklahoma and West Texas with my dad for ranch stuff."

"Love, love, love to travel." Pam raised her hand to her heart and leaned her head back, exposing a long neck that Jason instantly wanted to touch.

The effects of the rum loosened his inhibitions. "Oh, one time I did run to Little Rock after my sister got into some trouble." He leaned back in the rocker and smiled to himself at the memory of bailing Olivia out of jail. "She's always doing something to ruin someone else's day."

"I can't say that I've ever been to Little Rock," Pam admitted. "I have, however, been to Plymouth Rock, Balanced Rock, and the Rock of Gibraltar, but not Little Rock."

"Wow." Jason had never met anyone like Pam. This lovely lady seemed to have seen it all. "You do love to travel."

"My parents took me everywhere when I was growing up. They offered me the best experiences. Each spring break, Christmas break, and summer vacation, we found some new area to discover." Pam turned to Jason and repositioned herself so she could face him. She needed a better angle to watch his expression. "After we finished exploring the entire state of Colorado, we made it a goal to visit every national park in the United States."

"And? Did you reach your goal?"

"Almost. We have two more parks; Texas is our last state. I can't wait to get to Big Bend and Guadalupe Mountains."

Pink highlights on her cheeks made her smile softer and more genuine in Jason's eyes. *What I wouldn't do to have her lean one of those cheeks into the palm of my hand. The green of her eyes is so damned sexy. If I could just find a way to be closer.*

Jason convinced himself to bring his thoughts back to reality before the liquor talked him into reaching for her. "So, are you enjoying the house?" The only item out of place was a drill that Pam left lying on the edge of the middle step. Jason glanced at it. "Are you having any problems with anything?"

Pam followed his line of sight. "I love the house. It's absolutely perfect. I just need to tighten that one step. I got distracted by an impulse to paint a sunset, followed by Big Bird appearing in my yard.

Jason nodded, "I got you." He stood and let himself into the house like he owned the place.

Confused, Pam followed him through the back door and through the kitchen to the laundry room. The previous owner had left enough tools for Pam to take on almost any small project. She tilted her head as Jason opened the small closet, then squatted and searched through a drawer. He seemed to make himself at home in her house. "What are you—"

"It's right where I left it." Jason sensed tension coming from behind him and turned to face Pam. The look on her face made him grin. "I guess the realtor didn't tell you about the previous resident of this house?"

When Pam shook her head, he stood with a box of wood screws in his hand. "You didn't know that this place was mine before you bought it, did you?"

She shook her head again.

Jason walked past her, hiding a smile as he walked back through the house to the step that needed to be repaired. As he drilled two screws into the wood, he explained. "My dad built this house when he knew he was getting close to retiring. I moved in so I could be closer to the farm. When I took over the daily operations, he gathered what little he needed from the big house"—his thumb jutted over his shoulder to his house next door—"and moved into a tiny house at the far southwest corner of the property."

"So, I bought this house from you." Pam frowned. "You already know more about me than most people." With arms crossed over her chest, Pam admitted, "I don't know how to feel about that."

Open Bar

Friday, August 18, 2017

LARGE SPEAKERS STOOD tall beside the DJ stand and multi-colored lights flashed to the beat of Tim McGraw's "Down on the Farm." Couples two-stepped, guys pushed their girls in a circle, on the outside edge of the hardwood dance floor.

The Rockin' S Bar & Grill hosted more wedding receptions than any banquet hall west of Decatur. The owners specifically decorated the oversized room to accommodate those that chose a rustic wedding theme.

Award-winning barbecue attracted folks from all around the state. Various meats and sauces mingled to form the best scent in Jason's opinion; his stomach began to growl the moment he entered the bar.

It had only taken Tony Williams eleven years and a stern ultimatum before he popped the question to his high school sweetheart. Everyone knew they would end up together, but Lisa made it clear that the only way she would agree to give him children was if he gave her his last name first.

Because Jason didn't have a date for the wedding of one of his oldest friends, he arrived late to the reception. He had agreed to make an appearance but thought he would look and feel out of place if he attended the ceremony alone.

Nick Cain and his new wife, Samantha, graced one of the tables along the far wall; they waved Jason over to join them. Jason, Nick, and Tony had been inseparable during junior high and high school.

Now that it's official, the party can continue. Jason chuckled to himself as he made his way across the room. His friends had always been a little crazy; growing up in the country, there wasn't much to do besides find creative ways to get into trouble.

Weekends consisted of ATV four-wheeling when they were young; when they were old enough, Jeep mudding took over. For Tony and Nick, partying was second nature. Jason's mother had kept a close eye on her offspring and wouldn't hear of them whooping and hollering at the neighbor's weekly bonfire parties. Not to mention, his father whipped a mighty mean switch, so Jason wasn't privy to the early party days with his friends.

Brad and Greg Daniels, friends from neighboring Paradise, Texas, along with their dates had made the sixty-mile drive to celebrate the Williams' wedding. Their father was a cattle rancher and had shared best practices with Jason's father for years.

The boys met and became fast friends at an early age. Hell, Olivia had even tried to seduce Brad when she was a teenager. Brad, who had known she was trouble from day one, steered clear. The men had made it a point to stay in touch after each of them left the comfort of their parents' homes.

If only he had thought about asking Pam to accompany him to the reception—she would have been the perfect addition to the group of friends. He could almost see her on his arm, wearing a long flowing dress that made the bridesmaids gowns seem substandard. *Nah, she likes to be different. I bet she would wear a hot pink mini skirt with a tight white tank top. Something that would show off her thin-but-curvy frame.*

Most of the small town of Loving, Texas had been in attendance for the Williams' wedding. From the minister that performed the ceremony to the sheriff that had pulled Jason over last week just to give him a hard time for driving the speed limit, almost everyone played a role in his life. Except one lovely specimen alone at the bar.

With her back turned toward Jason, the lady's

somewhat familiar blonde hair fell over her bare shoulders. She turned to look down the bar and he caught a glimpse of her profile. The first word to enter his mind was "stunning."

Bluebonnets dotted her white halter dress and the material stretched tight across the upper half of her body. Only the lower half of her back was covered, leaving a strip of sun-kissed skin visible. Her tan, muscled calves stretched into white pumps. Jason allowed himself to visualize his hand tracing her curves from the inside of her ankle, behind her knee, up her thigh, and...

The lady threw her head back in laughter and Jason realized it was Pam, his neighbor, that filled the seat at the bar. Alone. *What luck!* He hadn't seen Pam all week. That wasn't to say he hadn't thought about how it would feel to hold her close and breathe in her succulent rose scent. *This could be one hell of a night.*

The bartender poured Pam another drink, adding an obvious wink. He leaned on one elbow and ran his finger under Pam's chin in an intimate gesture. She backed away and tilted her head down, acting shy, but the slow grin conveyed she enjoyed the attention.

Heat rose from Jason's neck to his ears; he paused to undo the strangling first button of his shirt before he approached the bar. *Dan's such a tool. Why is she hanging on his every word?*

After Jason adjusted his mindset and put on his best *I-couldn't-care-less* expression, he pulled his cowboy hat low over his brow and strolled to the bar. He leaned close behind the bar stool and whispered "Hey, babe," in Pam's ear.

Startled by the low raspy voice, her initial reaction had been annoyance but when she turned and recognized Jason's smirk, a lazy smile softened her eyes. "Hey, back."

As most bartenders tend to be, Dan was accustomed to a boyfriend showing up unexpectedly. Unsure of the relationship between Pam and Jason, he took a step back and lifted his chin in Jason's direction, "What can I get ya, friend?"

Jason laid a twenty-dollar bill on the bar, "Make another drink for the lady. I'll take a Dos Equis."

"Open bar." Dan pushed the twenty back and nodded before turning to fill the order.

With his arm across the back of Pam's chair, Jason wondered out loud, "What are you doing here?" Her shoulder radiated a warmth that Jason found hard to ignore. He gave in to the impulse to touch her skin and ran his fingers over her shoulder.

"I needed to break away from my latest painting." Pam shrugged. "It was getting too heavy. And, besides, my friends asked me to meet them at a super-casual wedding reception. I wasn't going to crash, but I finally said to myself, 'Self, why the hell not?'" Confidence lit a spark in Pam's eyes and she offered Jason a warm smile. "I assume you know Tony and Lisa?"

"I do. Tony's one of my best friends and I've known Lisa forever. Do you know them?"

"I've met Lisa a few times through my friends Grace and Danica." Pam leaned toward Jason to get a better view before she raised her arm and pointed to the opposite side of the room. "They're sitting at the loud table in the corner. I was just getting a drink before heading over to say hi."

The scent of her perfume tickled Jason's senses and he tried not to audibly inhale. "Would you care to join me for a dance first?" He held his hand out, palm up, toward Pam.

At first, she hesitated. She tilted her head and reminded herself that she wasn't looking for any kind of relationship. Always up for an adventure, she put her hand in his and smiled wide.

"Ah, what the hell, this could be fun." "Body Like a Backroad," Pam's new favorite song, started to play. She hopped off her perch at the bar and followed Jason's lead.

Once they reach the dance floor, Jason tugged on Pam's hand, spun her in a half-circle, and led her into the two-step position. An unexpected twinkle of surprise lit

Pam's eyes and she quickly fell into step in front of Jason.

A crooked smile and dark eyes peered out from under the rim of his cowboy hat. She attempted to hide the desire on her face but failed. Standing so close to the man of her fantasies for the last week proved to be more difficult that she thought it would be.

Less than six inches separated Jason from his gorgeous neighbor. As he watched her dance backward in high heels, his heart thumped inside his chest. He had to concentrate on the dance steps to squeeze out the intimate thoughts about touching her.

The tight muscles of Jason's bicep flexed under Pam's fingers and she felt herself inching closer. Or was she being guided by Jason's grip? Even though she told herself it was a bad idea to let the visions of him kissing her enter her thoughts, his lips captured her attention.

As if Jason could read her mind, he adjusted his stance and pulled her close. The dance steps had been burned in his memory by years of practice, so he moved on autopilot. A wry smile twisted his lips as Pam raised her eyes to his.

"Jason?"

Brown eyes flaked with gold stared down at Pam. "Mmm hmm." He didn't look away or speak. Once she was in his embrace, an air of confidence overtook him.

A shiver climbed up the back of her arms. She was

sure he knew exactly what he was doing and exactly what she was thinking. She praised herself for choosing a sundress as her temperature started to rise.

"You look gorgeous tonight," Jason whispered in her ear and then pressed his lips against her warm skin, just below her earlobe. He growled. "That dress is driving me crazy."

Heat from his breath in Pam's ear and the feel of his lips on her skin made her miss a step. She let out a short laugh when Jason led her in a quick turn as if the mistake had been intentional.

After he pulled her close again, she smiled and chose to enjoy being in the arms of a man instead of wondering what may or may not happen next. Even if he was her neighbor. It has been too long.

The next song brought line-dancers to the dance floor and the two separated. Pam expected Jason to sit this one out; instead, he stood beside her and moved his feet to the rhythm right along with the rest of the crowd.

Grace and Danica found Pam on the dance floor and slid into position beside their friend. Knowing looks between the three girls brought a blush to Pam's cheeks and she shrugged in response to unasked questions.

Tony and Lisa joined everyone in the line dance and the entire bar whooped and hollered. Once the groom dipped his bride and kissed her for the thousandth time that day, everyone erupted in applause.

∩ ∩ ∩

HORSES NICKERED at the humans when the barn door opened. It was past their feeding time and they reminded Jason that he was late. A black mare pawed at the door of her stall, her way to communicate annoyance. In the next stall, a tall bay mare stood wide-eyed until Jason cooed a greeting and caressed her neck.

"They're beautiful, Jason. I've always wanted to go horseback riding. Like, go for a real trail ride."

Surprised, Jason responded, "Of all people, I would have thought you would be an expert rider."

"Nope. My dad is afraid of animals this big. I never had the chance to learn about horses. Always wanted to. You know, the typical 'little girl enamored with horses' fantasy. Yeah, that was me."

Both horses continued their low nickers and Jason directed his attention to them. "Sorry, girls. I know I'm late." Grain had been scooped into individual bowls and slid under each stall door. "I blame this one." Jason pointed a thumb over his shoulder toward Pam.

"Hey, it's not my fault you wanted one more dance."

"It is absolutely your fault." Jason reached for Pam and pulled her close. "Apologize to my precious girls."

He stared into Pam's eyes, licked his lips, and brought them within a kissable distance.

Do I really want to start something with my neighbor? Pam thought. *Damn, that cowboy hat sure does look good on him. Girl you better get a grip.*

Pam took a deep breath, released it, and said, "Fine, fine." With sincerity in her voice, she spoke to the horses without taking her eyes off Jason. "Girls, I'm so sorry that your dinner is late. Mr. Jason, here, begged me for one more dance and I simply couldn't refuse."

With a roll of his eyes, Jason released her.

"Honkey Tonk Badonkadonk" played on the radio in the background and Jason laughed. He sang a couple of the lines and winked at Pam.

Pam swayed her hips to the beat and moved her feet, mimicking the line dance they'd shared earlier in the night. When she twirled, her sundress fanned out, showing her legs.

Pulled by desire, Jason sauntered over in her direction. When he was close enough, she grabbed the hat off his head and placed it over her blonde curls.

He let out a seductive groan and ran his hand through his hair. "Damn, girl. You're asking for trouble." In one swift move, he closed in on her and wrapped an arm around her waist. When their bodies touched, he spun her around and moved his hips with hers.

Unable to break the gaze they shared, Pam, now wearing his cowboy hat, rested one arm over Jason's shoulders. She placed her other hand in his and followed his lead as he two-stepped through the narrow opening of the barn. By the time the song ended, they were both out of breath, either from the dance or the electric connection between them. Neither knew which.

The anticipation of what could happen next thrilled Pam; she bit her lower lip and mirrored the expression on Jason's face, waiting with bated breath. Literally. These were the moments she lived for. She knew it couldn't be a great idea to become involved with her neighbor, but damn it, he was so freaking sexy.

He stared into her green eyes and fought to control the want—the need that engulfed his entire body.

Warmth from Jason's fingers splayed across the small of her back and sent a chill up her spine. She started to back away. After only three steps, she collided with the door to the tack room and her eyes widened.

Jason grinned when he understood that she realized there was no way to escape him. He trapped her in place with one hand on the wall beside her head and wrapped his other arm completely around her waist. "Trouble," he repeated and removed his cowboy hat from her head.

Pam's breath caught in her throat and her lips parted. Instinctively, she wrapped her arms around the cowboy's neck. "Am I?" she teased before his mouth covered hers. A whimper escaped Pam, causing Jason to tighten his grip and increase the passion of his kiss.

He gripped the back of her neck and angled her head to a position that allowed for the deepest kiss. He moved his other hand over her perfectly curved rear, her skirt gathered in his hand as he inched it up.

When his hot hand touched the tender skin of her thigh, Pam moaned and pressed her entire body against his. It was apparent that she was not the only one enjoying their connection. The obviousness of his excitement pleased her.

His lips traveled down her chin to her neck; she leaned her head back to allow easier access and laced one hand through his thick hair.

Just as Jason had fantasized earlier in the night, his hands found their way under her skirt. "Damn, woman." He found her mouth again, revealing his hunger.

Blindly, he guided her to stacked hay bales that were covered with a blanket beside the tack room. Their mouths parted just long enough for him to lift her onto the bales and position himself between her knees.

Dancing in the Rain

Saturday, August 19, 2017

BIRDS CHIRPED OUTSIDE Pam's bedroom window. The slight breeze moved the sheer curtains and brought with it the scent of Vitex trees that grew beside the house. She roused, smiling at the memory of the previous night, and opened her eyes. Expecting to find Jason lying beside her, Pam frowned at the empty bed.

Shit.

She took a deep breath and rolled to her back as she silently kicked herself for sleeping with her neighbor. *How awkward will it be to see Jason across the fence when I go out to my studio? What about when we both stop for lunch at the café, or pump gas, or end up at the Rockin' S again?* "Ugh. What have I done?"

The button-up shirt he wore to the wedding was draped over the chair in the corner of her room.

Is that the equivalent of a woman leaving her purse at a man's house just to have an excuse to see him again? She laughed at herself. "How 1990."

Pam remembered how warm his hands had been on her skin, how his lips and teeth tickled her neck, and the way he gazed into her eyes. If she looked in the mirror, she would probably find little bruises on her behind from his fingertips—the product of his enthusiasm when he'd realized she was wearing a thong.

The encounter had been filled with more passion than she had experienced in her life; the memory of it brought a smile to her lips and warmth to her core. *It was worth it, even if it was just for one night. We're both adults, right? We'll figure it out.*

Acting as the gentleman that his mother taught him to be, Jason offered to walk her home. She led him to her house and he began to kiss her outside the door. Their lips never parted as they crossed through the kitchen, through the dining room, up the stairs, and to her bed.

Even as they frantically removed each other's clothes, their lips remained fused as if no force on Earth could part them. Jason slowed their progression as they stood beside her bed. He held her so close they touched from knee to shoulder. "I don't want this to end. Let me love you."

Pam gasped as his lips covered hers and he lowered her to her lavender-scented sheets.

As Pam relived the scenes behind closed eyelids—kiss by kiss, touch by touch—again and again, she drifted back to sleep.

∩∩∩

"HEY, BABE." Jason's voice woke her. He trailed a finger from her shoulder to her wrist as he sat beside her on the bed.

"Mmm." A lazy smile spread across her lips. "You came back." When she opened her eyes, she could hardly believe that the fun-loving, goofy guy from next door had decided to return.

Jason grinned and handed her a mimosa. "Good morning, beautiful." Light from the late morning shone through the window, highlighting his five o'clock shadow.

"A girl could get used to this." Wrapped in a sheet, Pam wriggled up to lean against the headboard. "Thank you."

"No." With lifted eyebrows, Jason said, "Thank you. For a spectacular ending to what very well could have been an incredibly boring night. I'll never go to another wedding without remembering Tony and Lisa." He winked and lifted his glass in a toast. "To weddings."

Pam chuckled and clinked her glass to his. "To weddings." She slid over and made room for Jason to join her.

He accepted the extra pillow, propped it against the headboard and leaned back. "So, Miss Pam, tell me how you know Dan."

"Dan?" Pam squinted and shook her head, confused.

"Dan. The bartender. At Rockin' S."

Putting on her best flirty grin, she responded, "Oh, that Dan." *He almost sounds a little jealous.* "He's just a friend." She left the explanation hanging. It was amusing to realize that Jason became a little possessive. Just a little.

He didn't move the conversation to another subject, so she decided to ease his wariness.

"I met him at the bar when I first moved here. He was nice enough to give me a rundown on where to go in town for whatever I needed and which locals to stay away from. Day one, I made it clear that I wasn't interested. He's a nice guy, but that's all." She smiled to herself when Jason's shoulders relaxed, then decided to tease him, "However, I'm not sure I can say the same about someone else I just met."

"What? I'm not a nice guy?" He knew that wasn't

what she meant but put his hand on his heart and feigned a pain in his chest. "That's cold."

Pam rolled her eyes and laughed. "And for someone who thinks of himself as not very exciting, you sure can dance with the best of them."

Jason shrugged.

"I mean it—better than any other partner I've had." *In more ways than one.* Pam blushed at her own thought. "You can two-step anywhere, can't you? On the dance floor, in the barn, in the hay. How'd you get so good?"

"My momma always told me that cowboys that can't dance don't never catch them a good wife." Jason smiled at the memory. "I've never been much of a country music fan. I had to learn to dance to please my mom."

"We gave your girls a good show, didn't we?" Proud of herself for not being embarrassed, Pam waggled her eyebrows.

Jason caught Pam's hint and reached for her glass; he placed both on the nightstand and turned to Pam. Visions of the previous night fluttered through his memory. He moved toward her with a purpose, his expression serious. His lips fluttered over hers and he drawled, "Yeah, I think we may have ruined them."

One hot kiss followed another until Jason positioned her flat on the bed and covered her body with his.

Pam jumped up and grabbed the first piece of

clothing she could reach—Jason's button-up shirt that had been tossed over her chair. She didn't say anything and just rushed out the door.

Shocked by Pam's sudden departure, Jason paused and wondered if he'd misjudged the situation. He followed her out of the house to her studio. Once inside, he understood.

A fresh, extra-large canvas sat on the easel in front of Pam; a paintbrush was lodged in one hand and a palette with several colors of paint was in the other.

Captivated by her movements and not wanting to interrupt, he leaned against the counter on the far wall and watched. She had already outlined a cowboy hat in a deep brown.

Pam's strokes of the brush and her choice of colors flowed as if she were dancing or speaking a unique language. It seemed as though the world around her had disappeared.

The radio inside the small building had been tuned to a pop station and "Uptown Funk" started to play. Pam sang along and moved her hips to the beat. "This is my theme song, cowboy." A look over her shoulder invited him to join her.

Jason moved to stand behind her and put his hands on her hips, swaying along with the beat. He moved her blonde locks over one shoulder and traced the back of her neck with hot wet kisses. His hands wandered over her body and under her shirt.

With one hand, she reached over her shoulder and ran her fingers through his hair. She turned to face him and his mouth claimed hers; her eyes closed and she held her breath, not wanting the moment to end.

He paused, gazed into her eyes, and traced her jaw with the back of his fingers. "I've never met anyone like you. I'm infatuated."

Pam bit her bottom lip. "You do something to me that I can't explain."

Jason placed her on the edge of the counter and stood between her knees, allowing him to view every expression of passion on Pam's face as the situation progressed.

ロロロ

ANOTHER TYPICAL Saturday night for the small group of ladies started with a couple of beers and then graduated to mixed drinks at The Rockin' S bar. Half-full glasses of Angry Orchard mixed with Fireball shots sat in front of the three friends. They let go of built-up stress from the previous work week as stories soon turned to gossip.

Raindrops landed on the metal roof like horse hooves pounding the ground in a gallop. Pam's eyes widened and a smile decorated her lips. "Come on!" She grabbed Grace's hand from across the table and practically pulled her out the door to the covered porch.

Always up for a good time, Danica egged Pam on as she followed them outside. She noticed a streak of purple peeking out under Pam's short shorts. "Hey, girl. What's with the paint on your ass?"

"What?" Pam twirled in a circle as she tried to get a look at her backside. She got dizzy and grabbed the railing for support. Laughing, she shrugged. "Eh, just had a little fun with my neighbor in the studio earlier."

"Shut up!" Danica punched her in the arm a little harder than she meant to and apologized. "Dude, you need to spill. That boy is too hot."

Anxious to cool off in the rain, Pam dismissed the request. "Later. Let's go."

"Damn it, Pam! It took me half an hour to get my hair just right." Even though she pretended to be annoyed, Grace grinned as she bounced down the steps.

"And it will take five seconds for the rain to ruin it." Danica allowed the adrenaline to take over as she followed her friends to a small patch of grass near the parking lot. This wasn't the first time they had wandered into a storm and surely wouldn't be their last; a crowd formed around the girls just like last time.

Speakers on the outside of the building pumped

country music into the night. The girls sang along with Toby Keith, raised their hands, shook their hips, and allowed the alcohol to provide some extra courage. Even though the dance floor inside was professionally polished, and totally dry, the best area to observe the fun was in the rain.

Pam had pulled her hair into a ponytail before the rain soaked her; she looked just as good after the dance as before it. Some might have said that she looked even better wet. Her pale blue shirt clung to her chest and belly, showing the details of her lacy undergarment.

After two songs, they went back inside and accepted a towel from the bartender. "Y'all are crazy, I tell ya." Dan shook his head and chuckled as he filled three shot glasses with Fireball.

Cool air from the air conditioning gave Pam chills: she needed to warm up and downed the drink. "Think T-bone is ready for a ride?" She slammed her empty glass on the bar and turned toward the mechanical bull. Over her shoulder, she smiled wide and called to the bartender. "Turn it up, Dan."

"Courtesy of the Red, White, and Blue" blared out of the juke as Pam stepped into the ring with T-bone. She threw a leg over the mechanical bull and held tight to the makeshift handle.

One of the waitresses controlled the machine from a

near-by table and laughed along with the girls as Pam fell to the vinyl air mattress.

"My turn!" Danica traded places with Pam. "I bet I can beat your time."

"Hey, gorgeous." One of the men that sat at a table near the corral had watched Pam ride and blocked her path as she tried to pass. He lifted his chin. "The names Franklin. You're not only pretty, you're pretty good."

She squinted her eyes, tilted her head, and almost spat the words. "The name's not Gorgeous. But thanks." Then she turned and walked in the other direction to stand beside Grace. It was tradition to cheer on Danica as she tried again and again to beat Pam's time.

"Never fails, girl." Grace chuckled and shook her head. "You sure know how to attract the good ones."

Pam rolled her eyes and ignored the stares from the neighboring table.

The stranger appeared beside Pam, gripped her shoulder, and turned her around. "Wanna dance, blondie?"

"No." The scent of whiskey mixed with cigarettes wafted through the air and turned Pam's stomach. She didn't bother to elaborate.

"Ah, come on. After we're done, you can drape those blonde curls over my…"

"Are you deaf? I said no. Now buzz off." Pam

strained to make herself heard over the loud music, turned away, and attempted to wind between tables. The bar was crowded, leaving no space between chairs and no escape route.

It only took a couple steps for Franklin to catch up to her. "No chick turns their back on me." He slurred his words and took a step closer. His fingers wrapped around her bicep, forcing her to stop.

Pulling strength from the loud crowd and liquor, Pam shook loose of his grip. She placed her hands on her hips and stood tall. "I said no, loser. And don't touch me again."

She laughed off the close call and led her friends to the dance floor. Just when she had gotten into the groove, she felt someone dancing close to her backside. She moved away and looked over her shoulder. It was him.

Franklin gripped her hips and pulled her to him. Unable to break his hold this time, Pam tensed.

He growled in her ear. "Women don't ever deny me. Ever."

Jerks at the bar had always been part of the scene and Pam was rarely intimidated, but this guy was different. Something about his energy felt off, almost vengeful, Disgusted, she squirmed. "I said don't touch me. Fuck off."

A short blonde lady that Pam had never seen stood

before her, screaming obscenities—something about her husband. Then, a pain in her eye caught her off guard and everything moved in slow motion.

The music stopped and the entire bar fell quiet. All eyes were on the two women on the dance floor. Pam didn't think. Her instincts took over and she threw a jab that landed square on the bitch's nose.

The short lady's body twisted; her blonde hair spun out around her face like a fan, her arms fell limp, and her knees buckled. As she hit the floor, a sound like thunder after a bright burst of lightning filled Pam's ears.

Bright red streaks of blood spattered across the dance floor and the lady's body lay sprawled out like a scene in a murder mystery.

"What the hell?" Pam asked out loud and her right hand started to pulse. O*ne and done. KO for the win.* She smiled to herself and sauntered to the bar for another shot.

Shiners

Sunday, August 20, 2017

SHADES OF BLUE, PINK, purple, and orange spread across the canvas in yet another depiction of a Texas summer sunset. One reason Pam decided not to go back to Colorado was the fantastic colors that naturally paint the sky. She told her friends that she couldn't resist trying to reproduce the superb colors.

As usual, Pam's mood reflected in her art. Even though her head pounded from both the liquor and the punch, she had been overcome with the sense of strength and freedom.

After crawling into bed at four-o-clock in the morning, she found it difficult to sleep. The fight, if you could call it that, replayed in a loop in her mind.

When she decided to roll out of bed, the reflection in her mirror had startled her and she cringed. "Well, look what the cat dragged in."

Hours later in her studio, Pam heard a faint whistle above the quiet music playing on her radio. She cocked an ear toward the sound as it grew stronger.

Dammit, I just got into a groove. A frown covered her face; she wondered if the sound itself annoyed her or the fact that Jason could do something she couldn't do. She gave up trying to perfect whistling years ago.

Pam peered out the window over the counter where she sat in paint the day before; the memory of how Jason touched and kissed every inch of her brought heat to her cheeks. Pleased at the sight of her sexy neighbor approaching, she failed at the attempt to push away her headache. In his hands were a bottle of wine and a bouquet of summer flowers.

Still a little hungover from the shots of Fireball and her cheek pulsating where that little shit's punch connected, she chuckled as she remembered the hussy slumped on the floor.

Jason knocked twice and cracked the door. "Hey, babe. You in there?"

Pam opened the door completely and grinned; an all-out smile would have been too painful.

He gasped and set the gifts on a table. "Pam, what's with the shiner?" He gently ran his fingertips over the bruise on her eye and kissed her on the lips as if it were the most natural reaction. "Are you ok? Who did this to you?" He framed her face with his hands, only touching one cheek, as he studied the growing purple, pink, and blue area.

"It's nothing," a shrug dismissed the significance of the injury. "You should see the other girl." She sniggered and hugged Jason.

With one arm, he instinctively pulled her close, placed a kiss in her hair, and whispered in her ear, "Looks like you could use a drink." He backed away and winked.

"Ah, nothing like the hair of the dog," Pam agreed. The label on the bottle didn't look familiar. "Where is this from? Is it local?"

"I got this from a winery outside of Sunset last year." He opened the wine and poured the cool, sweet, clear substance into two plastic cups. "Our group knows the owners of Marker Cellars, great people. We like to support our local businesses and they have great wines and ciders."

"That's great. I would love to go there sometime. I just love wineries." Pam lifted her glass in a toast. "To?"

"To winning."

A wince accompanied Pam's smile as she drank. "Mmm. Is that honey I taste? This is just lovely. Thanks, Jason."

"Wow, Pam." An image behind Pam caught his eye

and he adjusted his stance so he could look at the painting on the opposite wall. "When did you finish that one?" He stole a quick glance in her direction. "Was that here last night?"

"No. I finished that one this morning."

"It's beautiful—breathtaking. You have such talent, I'm so impressed." Because it wasn't completely dry, Jason resisted running his fingers over the landscape, a sunset with bluebonnets in the foreground. A rancher stood at one side of the canvas with his hands on his hips and his head bowed. A small mound of dirt rose out of the flowers, a cross stuck in the ground.

"Is that…" His voice trailed off and he leaned closer to the painting and squinted, really looking at it. He read the name painted on the cross, "Rocky?" He turned and captured Pam's gaze. "That's me standing next to Rocky's grave, isn't it?"

Pam nodded.

"I can feel the emotion you poured onto this canvas. Pam, not just see it." Jason reached out and enveloped her. "Thank you. You have no idea how much this means to me," he whispered in her ear.

One hand rested on the back of her neck as he placed a kiss beneath her earlobe. His lips traced the outline of her jaw on the way to her mouth.

Her arms wrapped around his waist and she pulled

him close, reveling in the warmth of his embrace. His soft lips covered hers and he breathed his love into her.

A different form of desire filled Jason; the desire to know this beautiful woman. A desire to open his heart to her. He broke the kiss and placed a hand on her good cheek. She leaned into his palm exactly as he had fantasized.

"I want to know everything about you; you're so interesting. I feel a connection that's both electric and soothing. Does that make any sense?" He never thought he would say such things so quickly after meeting someone, but he couldn't resist.

Pam placed a sensual but soft kiss on his lips. When she looked into his dark eyes, she smiled and nodded. "I wasn't looking to have any kind of relationship with anyone more than just being friends. I was happy just getting out and meeting people."

Jason grinned and waited for her to continue.

"The connection is undeniable, for sure. I have to tell you that it's very unlike me to move as quickly as I did Friday night." Searching his eyes for understanding, she said, "I always make it a point to wait at least a couple months before getting physical, so I usually get to know someone first. I've never done anything this soon with a boyfriend."

The minute the word *boyfriend* came out of her

mouth, Jason smiled wide. He interrupted her. "Does that mean you're my baby girl?"

Pam nodded and let out a giggle. "And you'll be my cowboy."

TWO HOURS LATER, Pam walked up the steps to Jason's back door. She ran her hand over the back of each cat within reach and cooed her greeting, a lazy grin on her lips.

The screen door stood open and Jason invited her inside. He led her to the kitchen where he had begun to prepare an early dinner. "You sure you're okay hanging out with my sister and her husband tonight?"

"Sure." Pam shrugged. "What's the worst that could happen?"

"Great." He kissed her nose. "We agreed that Sunday evenings should be spent with family at the homestead." A hint of disappointment flickered in Jason's eyes. "Even if Dad refuses to join us." Changing the subject before she could ask any questions, he nodded toward Pam. "So, tell me what really happened?"

She leaned against the counter and placed one hand over her heart. "Whatever do you mean?" Her sarcasm obvious.

"The shiner." Jason lifted one hand in amusement.

"It all happened so fast," Pam explained. "I guess it started when I rode T-bone."

"What? Who's T-bone?" Jason's brows formed a V, causing Pam to laugh.

"T-bone is the name I gave the mechanical bull."

Jason shook his head and chuckled. "Okay."

"I had a pretty good ride and when I finished, some jerk started hitting on me. I made it clear that I wasn't interested, but he kept pushing me. To make a short story shorter, he followed me to the dance floor, grabbed me by the waist, and started grinding into my backside. I turned to break his hold and my face met some bitch's fist."

"Jesus."

"Yeah. I swung; she fell. The end." Pam shrugged. "This morning, after I took a shower, cleared my head, and walked to my studio, I really began to wonder what it all meant. I'm still so confused about it all."

Heat from the oven breezed through the small kitchen as Jason put the cheesy potato bake inside. He set the timer and pulled a soda stream machine to the edge of the counter.

"Are you sure I can't help?" It made Pam uncomfortable to let someone else do all the work.

"Nope. All I need you to do is stand there and look pretty." He winked. "Would you like some of my magic lemonade?"

"I'd love some, thanks. What makes it magical?"

He didn't answer but nodded to the carbonating device. Country Time powder had been added to the container prefilled with water. Confidence radiated through Jason's goofy expressions. He wiggled his eyebrows and moved his hands like a magician, presenting the container as the 'before,' while he screwed the bottle into the fancy machine.

Once he pressed the button, the machine produced a horrific sound, screeched, and then liquid exploded across the room. Jason squealed as he released the button and swore. Last time this happened, he promised himself he would remember that he needed to add the powder after he carbonized the water.

Pam laughed at the sound that reminded her of the day they met. "Oh, my god, you sound like a little girl." The more she thought about the squeal, the more she laughed. Doubled over, tears began to run down her cheeks. "Oh, my face hurts."

"Awe, shit." Wet towels had been spread across the floor and he dried the counter with wadded paper towel.

As Jason cleaned the mess, he sighed. "My mom would kill me if she saw what I just did to her brand-new floor. Now it's going to be sticky for days."

"I can picture her scolding you." Pam giggled, then

a vision of Jason's mom smiling down at a ten-year-old boy filled her mind. "Did she teach you to dance here?" She put some soap on the wet paper towels and squatted next to Jason.

"Some. Not on this floor, though. Back then, it was a hideous yellow linoleum." A crooked grin formed on his lips. "The music she listened to all sounded the same back then. The songs were all so depressing. 'My wife left me,' or 'my dog ran away,' or 'my truck died.'" Lost in a memory, he paused. He smiled softly and his gaze seemed far away.

Once the spill had been cleaned, Pam pulled out a chair and sat at the table. "Tell me about her."

Jason joined her and leaned on his elbows. "She passed away five years ago now. Just three days after her forty-second birthday. Cancer took her super young."

"Oh, Jason," Pam reached forward and placed her hand on his arm. "I'm so sorry."

"Yeah. Me too." After a sigh, he continued, "I have the best memories of her. She made the best pies, always had a smile on her face, and smelled of vanilla." He chuckled and shook his head. "I just remembered that my dad used to ask me if I thought she used the vanilla from the baking cabinet as perfume. For the longest time, I thought she did.

"I excelled in 4-H because of her. My dad taught me

about all the animals and how they need different care, but my mom taught me about how to treat them. How to communicate with them. How to hear them. She also taught me how to sew. In my junior year, I had a home economics class and won a first-place award for sewing a pillow."

Pam's eyes widened.

"With ruffles."

She laughed.

"I asked the teacher to please give the award to the girl that came in second place. If she announced that I won during the last day of school awards banquet, I would never have lived it down."

"Jason, she sounds amazing. I wish I could have met her."

The sound of Pam's voice soothed Jason. "Me too." He lifted her hand to his lips and kissed the back of it. "She always put us first. She made it a point to get together with her friends who had kids the same age as me and my sister, Olivia, so we could play. If we weren't jumping on someone's trampoline, we would be on a pontoon at the lake. Summers seemed to last for so long back then.

"When we got older, our moms turned us loose; the girls would go play with dolls or cats or horses and us boys would get lost for hours on four-wheelers and dirt bikes." Changing the subject, he asked, "What about you? How did you spend your time growing up?"

"You were lucky to have a sister," Pam admitted. "I always wanted one. My mom said that God wanted her and my dad to only have me. I didn't know what that meant for a long time, so I thought she was making up some lame excuse. I was lucky in a different way, though. My parents did everything with me and took me everywhere. I learned how to have conversations with adults and keep myself occupied. I did not learn how to share." She lifted an eyebrow.

"I told you about travelling, that was my entertainment. There wasn't just one lake, or one sand dune, or one beach. We visited all of them. I didn't have many friends because we spent most of the summer somewhere other than Boulder. I wouldn't trade any of those experiences for the world, though.

"My mom and dad still live in my childhood home and practically begged me to come back after I dumped my ex. They taught me to be self-reliant and to be comfortable alone, so I figured I would give this beautiful state a real Texas try. I spent most of my time teaching one-off painting classes, so I figured I could find somewhere up here to teach and maybe sell some art in the DFW area."

Jason raised his eyebrows and smiled, "I didn't know

you taught. That's so cool. What do you mean by one-off classes?"

"You've heard of Painting with a Twist, or Paint and Pour, or Arty Party?"

A shake of his head told Pam he hadn't.

"Well, my little business is called Passion in the Paint. A restaurant or winery supplies the drinks or wine and I show up with canvases, paints, and brushes and teach people the basics of painting while they drink. I'll market ahead of time with two specific pictures and people choose which date they want to book based on which painting I'm teaching. It's pretty good money, honestly. It's enough to keep me going, anyway. Other than that, I have some paintings in a few galleries; I've sold a few."

The timer buzzed.

"Seriously, what can I do to help?" Pam stood.

"Set the table?"

Pam busied herself with perfecting the place settings at the table in the dining room, complete with flowers in a vase.

A jaguar pulled up the drive and Jason walked to the back door to greet his other guests. Low voices reverberated through the room and Pam's stomach began to flip. She told herself that this was nothing serious—just dinner. *It doesn't really mean anything. Yet.*

"Shit! Oh, my god, Liv! What the hell happened to you?"

Olivia glared past her brother as she processed the fresh memory. "Some slutty whore tried to get it on with Douglas at the Rockin' S last night, so I kicked her ass. No biggie."

Jason pursed his lips in understanding. Lowering his voice and his head, he repeated, "Shit."

Once Olivia entered the kitchen and saw Pam leaning against the counter, she nearly lost her mind. "What the hell is she doing here? Why is this whore in our house? How do you even know her, Jason?" Not waiting for an answer to any of her questions, Olivia moved across the room and stood close enough to Pam that she could smell her perfume.

Indifferent, Pam crossed her arms across her chest and lifted her chin. "Nice shiner." It was impossible to hide her pleasure while observing her own handy work.

Olivia squinted her eyes and her face turned red. "You need to leave. I'm not spending a single second with some sleazy slut that tried to sleep with my husband."

"What? Franklin?" She nodded toward Douglas who stood with his mouth agape. "No way would I ever try to get with that tool. You've got your story mixed up, darlin'; he started hitting on me the second I walked past his table. Even patted my ass. I blew him off, but he came after me."

All eyes focused on Pam and she realized that she was outnumbered.

Olivia glanced over her shoulder and asked, "Who's Franklin?" Her husband, Douglas, shrugged and shook his head.

"Um, Franklin, the man you came here with?" Pam pointed to the man that practically assaulted her the previous night. "Your so-called husband." She pushed away from the counter and the dramatic blonde in search of a less-crowded space.

Pam needed to get away from the situation but didn't want Jason to think she had done the things that Olivia described. His squinted eyes and tilted head told her that he didn't know who to believe.

"Are you delusional?" Olivia followed her like a Chihuahua chasing a treat.

Pam nodded in understanding, "Ah, fake name. Good one. Franklin or Douglas, whatever your name is. Will you please tell your wife the truth?"

"He didn't even notice you until you picked up his beer and started drinking it. When he asked what you were doing, you told him he needed to buy you a drink." Turning to her husband, Olivia said, "Right, honey?"

"Oh, my god. You weren't even there." Pam turned her back to the spectacle and faced Jason. The confusion in his eyes made her take a deep breath. "This is so messed up. I'm sorry, Jason. I didn't know the crazy chick that picked a fight with me was your sister. Enjoy your dinner. I'll see you later."

Olivia followed Pam toward the back door, grasped her bicep, and turned her around so they stood face to face; she wasn't finished with her yet. She didn't like to lose. "The entire bar saw you feeling up every man on the dance floor, grinding with them like you were the top-paid actress in *Dirty Dancing*."

Twisting out of Olivia's grasp, Pam clenched her fists in preparation to defend herself. Again. "Girl, you got some really bad intel."

Olivia moved to stand beside her husband. She jabbed him in the ribs until he spoke.

"That's right, she came on to me," Douglas backed his wife's story with a shaky voice. "She was all over me. Even tried to sit in my lap and ran her hands through my hair. Said something about being on top."

Now, Pam's mouth dropped. She couldn't believe such an intricate lie could be made up on the spot. She had been pretty drunk, so she began to question her memory. "Look, Jason, I may have had too much to drink and I may not remember every detail from last night, but I certainly did not hit on this guy. What I told you earlier was the honest-to-god's truth."

Confused and unsure which story to believe, Jason

put his hands up, palms out, and admitted, "This is all just too much drama for me." He ran one hand through his hair, then down his face. His eyes found Pam's and his voice trembled. "I don't think us being together was such a great idea."

Bamboozled

Tuesday, August 22, 2017

THE TWO-HOUR DRIVE to Frisco seemed to fly by. Pam wondered if it would be smart to spend the day with her friends if her heart wasn't in it. The last couple of days, she'd searched for a solution to her most recent conundrum: her complex relationship with Jason.

Grace and Danica had taken the day off work so they could spend a girl's day adventure with Pam; it didn't feel right to cancel.

Tuesday was the slowest day at iFLY, an indoor skydiving simulator; the girls had been excited to have an entire day together. A mini vacation, as Grace called it.

Even though Pam focused on the traffic, her mind continued to wander back to the interaction with Jason and his sister. *What the hell happened? Doesn't he feel what I'm feeling? He said we had an undeniable connection; he's not wrong. We just claimed each other a few hours before...Olivia. Why didn't he believe me?*

After Jason said what they shared had been a mistake, Pam's legs went weak. Unable to believe her own ears, she'd hesitated, staring at Jason. He turned his back to her. That was what hurt the most; he couldn't even look at her.

When she turned to walk out Jason's back door, she said to herself, "That did not just happen" before heading directly to her studio.

She opened her favorite bottle of wine and placed a blank canvas on her easel. The rest of the night, she refilled her plastic cup and layered various shades of red and orange mixed with black. White highlights made the details pop. She seemed to create the image without thought.

The end result, to her surprise, was a sunset with a silhouette of a man—a cowboy—sitting on his horse as the horse walked away from the barn. Bison dotted the landscape beyond a fence. It was obvious Jason had a strong hold on her.

At the end of the night, Pam's tears mixed with red splotches of paint on her cheeks. The wine bottle sat empty beside a full cup when she walked away. Defeated, she sank into her bed and into a deep sleep.

Tears stung her eyes again, at the thought of losing

Jason forever. She had been so sure that he would be the man to fill her days with joy and add excitement to the hot Texas summer nights.

Once Pam found a parking spot at the iFLY, she pulled the visor down and looked at her reflection in the mirror. Her eyes, still puffy from crying the night before, looked better after a touch-up of makeup. She sighed. "Good enough."

Wearing her best fake smile, Pam entered the building, found her friends, and greeted them with a hug. "Hey, Danica. Grace. I'm so excited for today. This is going to be so fricking fun!"

Right away, Danica noticed something off about Pam's demeanor and as their friend went to sign in, she asked Grace if she saw it too. Oblivious, Grace shook her head. "Nah, she's fine."

"No, I don't think she is. Her smile wasn't right." Danica leaned closer to Grace so Pam wouldn't overhear their conversation. "She's got something going on. I can tell. She needs us."

Because the simulator was very detailed and the instructors kept to a tight schedule, the girls paid attention to the instructions and focused on the flight. They could have this discussion later.

∩∩∩

CRAFTWAY KITCHEN, one of the best restaurants in Frisco, only had a short wait by the time the girls arrived for lunch. Their appetites had been increased by the adventure; the three were famished.

Plastic menus showcased sandwiches with a twist, making Danica's stomach growl. "Sorry, y'all. A cooter board isn't going to satisfy me this time. I need a Reuben today. Substance."

"Agree. Grilled salmon BLT for me," Grace said.

"The whitefish sounds good. I think I'm going to have that," Pam added.

A waiter dressed in black pants and a white button-up shirt took their order before he backed away with a wink in Grace's direction.

"Do you know him, Grace?" Danica asked with wide eyes.

"Maybe." A giggle spread around the table and the friends became reminiscent of the day's event.

"Did you ever think, four months ago, when we started hanging out, that we would all go skydiving?" Still on a high from flying, Grace smiled and practically bounced in her chair. "The second I stepped into the wind tunnel, my focus went from all the bullshit of my daily work drama to, I don't know. Freedom, I guess."

It would surely take days for her smile to fade. "The

feeling of floating"—she closed her eyes—"was like nothing I had ever experienced. It was like a fairy lifted me out of this dreadful world for a few minutes and showed me what it felt like to be her. I want to be as free as a fairy; I want to do this again. Like, tomorrow."

Amused as always with Grace's innocence and unique view of life, Danica laughed. "You're right, Gracie. It felt like freedom. Your fairy friend didn't accompany me, though. Besides the instructor, I was alone. Just me. When I closed my eyes, all my fears disappeared. All my anxiety about what life may or may not hold for me—gone. Just imagine what skydiving, for real would be like. Twelve thousand times as intense."

"Yeah, it was great." Pam attempted to appear excited but failed. The descriptions of her friend's experience made sense to her, but when she lifted into the air, she'd missed Jason. The instructor held her in place and offered security and safety, just like Jason had. During the short flight, Pam couldn't hold back the tears. She tried to explain it as excitement, but her friends knew better.

Danica, the bolder of the two, offered compassion to Pam since her despair was obvious. She leaned forward and put her forearms on the table. "Honey, what's wrong?"

Pam shook her head and mumbled, "It's nothing. I'm

good." She looked at Danica with sad eyes and tried to smile. Fighting the tears that threatened to form for the thousandth time, she added, "It's fine, I'm fine, everything's fine."

"We're friends Pam. You can talk to us, we're here to listen. That's what we do. We help, we offer advice, we make sure you're ok. Then, if need be, we kick someone's ass."

Grace giggled again and Pam's smile turned from forced to genuine.

"Okay, okay." Pam gazed beyond the tables and chairs and sighed. "I told you a little about having some fun with my neighbor, right?"

"The paint-on-your-ass guy?" Danica asked.

"Yeah." The memory brought a half-smile to Pam's lips. "So, we've spent some time getting to know each other and he's really great. He's been in Texas his entire life, loves animals. He's funny, sexy as hell, and so sweet."

"And?" Danica pushed when Pam paused and fiddled with her silverware.

"And it turns out that the chick that attacked me at the bar…" Lifting her gaze to Danica, she paused for effect. She widened her eyes and leaned forward. "Is his sister."

"Holy shit!" Grace covered her mouth with her

fingers.

"What?" Danica asked at the same time.

"I know right. Isn't that the weirdest thing? So anyway, can you believe he invited me over for dinner to meet his family? Well to meet his sister and her husband, which is the jackass that was trying to hit on me, and we had a confrontation. Jason believed them. They flat out called me a liar and said that I was trying to sleep with him." She brushed her hands together and sat back in her chair, "Done. Relationship over." She pursed her lips. "Well, if you could call it that."

"Of course, he believes her; she's his sister. Big brothers stick up for little sisters, no matter what. Not that it's the right thing to do, but that's what happens." Grace clasped her hands in front of her, "How can you prove to him that they're lying? And how can we help you?"

Pam sighed; her shoulders drooped. "Is it worth it? I mean we've only been together couple times."

Grace finally put the details together. "Oh my god! You slept with your neighbor."

Danica elbowed Grace in the ribs. "Hello, who did you think 'Paint-on-your-ass guy' was?" To Pam, she said, "Who cares who he is. You felt something. There's a connection, right?"

Silence and the sadness in her eyes spoke volumes.

"Of course, it's worth fighting for. Even though we

haven't known each other very long, I know you don't hop in bed with just anyone. You must have something going on in that big ol' heart of yours."

"I totally didn't expect it to hurt this much when he decided to stop seeing me. I mean, it's not like he's the first guy who didn't get me. Honestly, I didn't really think that this would be a long-term relationship. I kind of knew not to get into something with my neighbor, but damn it, he's just so sexy. He. Is. Exceptional," Pam enunciated. "And funny and clumsy and goofy and I just love him."

"You what?" Grace picked up on the "L" word immediately.

"What?" Pam frowned, confused why her friends gave her oogle eyes.

Danica nodded. "You just said you love him."

"No, I…" In denial, Pam shook her head.

A wide smile spread across Grace's perfectly painted lips. "Pam and Jason sitting in a tree," she sang.

"Oh, come on." An overexaggerated sigh and an eye roll had been used to attempt to hide Pam's smile. Grace always could make her chuckle.

Pam was finally ready to admit it out loud. "Damn it why do I have to fall for my neighbor? Oh, I just don't know what to do." She put her face in her hands. "We're so different but that doesn't mean the connection isn't there. It totally is.

"Before the dinner, we agreed to be together. Exclusive. I said the word boyfriend and he called me his baby girl."

Grace squealed and clapped her hands.

"But now…" Pam sighed, "Now it's meaningless. To be honest, I wasn't looking for anything serious, and after what just happened, I don't know if I want to be with someone right now. I just moved here, broke up with an asshole not very long ago; I still need to get past that." She met Danica's gaze. "Right?"

Kind eyes reflected her image, but her friend remained silent.

Pam continued, "Why wouldn't I date random people? Find out who I feel comfortable with and who gives me butterflies? And who doesn't. There are thousands of potential bachelors in the DFW area. I've been asking myself why I would jump into bed with the first one.

"What a stupid mistake. Now I have to make the best of an awkward situation. I'm going to have to at least go talk to him and tell him that it's fine and that there's no hard feelings."

The pain in Pam's eyes and her body language showed Danica that it was not fine. "Pam, how long are you going to beat yourself up for the wrong reason? It's obvious that you have feelings for this guy even if it's only been a couple weeks."

She leaned forward and captured her friend's attention. "What if the universe put you in that house? What if you were supposed to meet Jason and you were supposed to be with him. What if the connection with him is so strong because it's right?" She leaned back in the chair to let her words permeate.

When Pam raised her eyes, Danica grinned. "Maybe you shouldn't overthink it. Don't talk yourself out of a good thing."

"You know what?" Pam acknowledged both ladies that sat opposite her. "You're right. You're absolutely right." An honest smile adorned her face for the first time in days. "Thank you for helping me sort out what I want, what I need. There certainly is something to be said about clarity. I know what I need to do."

"SHE'S JUST SO different. We don't have anything in common. She's been everywhere and done almost everything. Like my dad said—"

"What?" Tony interrupted. "You're not seriously going to let your dad convince you what type of person you should date, possibly fall in love with, and spend a lifetime building a family and a legacy with, are you?"

Jason focused on the toe of his boot and frowned at the words that he had thought himself, but hadn't made sense until someone else spoke them out loud. "He's not wrong."

"Maybe, but he's also not right. He doesn't have a right to tell you how to feel. He's been through a lot of loss in his young life, but he shouldn't be holding you back because he's afraid to lose you too."

"Wow. That kinda makes sense."

Nick smiled. "I saw you dancing with her, and I know you haven't danced in way too long. After ol' what's her name turned you off anything country, music, dancing, clothes, you haven't been the true you. It's been years."

He waited until Jason glanced up and caught his gaze. "This girl, Pam, has a real hold on you and I can tell that you are the most comfortable you've been in your own skin a really long time."

"Yeah, but she's—"

"But nothin'," Tony interrupted. "Stop making excuses, man. For once in your life, Jason, do what you want to do. Not what your dad, or your friends, or anyone else wants you to do. Do what YOU want to do."

Brown Sugar Peach Cobbler

Wednesday, August 23, 2017

NERVES CAUSED PAM'S hands to shake as she applied eye shadow and liner to accentuate her green eyes. She hadn't made this much of a fuss over a guy for as long as she could remember. Either it was right at the time or it wasn't; uncertainty was not a normal emotion for her. She tousled her blonde curls and sprayed her hair one last time.

Dressed in a light pink shirt and white shorts, Pam's intention was to incite compassion and love. Her shirt fell off one shoulder and flowed around her waist; in contrast, the shorts hugged her. After a final swipe of pale pink lip gloss, she smiled at her reflection. She was ready to fight for Jason's heart.

Doubtful that he was expecting company, she hoped

he would be home and give her the time she needed to apologize and explain. She placed a bottle of Jefferson's Reserve whiskey, his favorite, and a small batch of brown sugar peach cobbler behind a chair on his porch. Behind her back, she held a small painting of a bison grazing in the sunset.

Jason appeared before she had a chance to knock. He paused and started through the screen door from across the room. The lady that had stolen his heart, then stomped on it, stood in front of him. Memories of their first night together, along with their passionate moment in the paint, clouded his thinking. His eyes roamed over her body longer than he'd intended.

With her hair pulled off her shoulders, Jason envisioned tracing his lips over her neck. Her lightweight shirt blew in the breeze, showing a strip of skin above her shorts.

Even though he wasn't touching her, Jason could feel the warmth of her waist on his palms. He could almost smell the rose-scented perfume she loved and hear her throaty laugh. If her intention was to appeal to all his senses at once, it worked.

Although he fought the urge to grin, he had been reluctant to let her in. He was still upset that she could be so violent, not only to someone in his family but to anyone, really.

The conversation with his friends about going after what he wanted made sense at the time, but he had to admit he and Pam were just too different. Even if they were physically compatible, that could only take them so far.

"What are you doing here?" Jason asked as he approached the screen door. He didn't open it or invite Pam inside.

She showed him the painting. "I made this for you. Can we talk?"

He hesitated, then opened the door and invited her inside. They walked to the sitting area off the dining room and chose chairs opposite each other.

"Listen, I don't want this to be any more difficult than it needs to be." Jason avoided her eyes and focused on a magazine on the coffee table. "I just don't know how I can be with someone that gets in bar fights." He shook his head and lifted his gaze to Pam. "Besides, we want different things out of life; you want to travel the world and try all kinds of wild, weird things. You long for adventure and I'm just a simple country boy that wants to live a peaceful, happy life. It just doesn't make sense—we don't make sense. I don't see how it can work. I hope you understand." Glad that was over, Jason leaned back in the chair and exhaled.

All her past relationships seemed to end with

"You're too adventurous," like that was a bad trait. She understood what Jason said—that they were different—but couldn't fathom why that should keep them apart. Besides, Jason fit her every need, unlike anyone else in her past and she refused to give up so easily.

Jason stood and turned.

"Jason." The sound of his name on her lips gave her strength. "I've listened to what you had to say. Can you please take a moment to hear me out? Don't I at least deserve that much?" She tilted her head, secretly pleading for him to recognize the passion in her voice. "If you care about me even a little, and I think you do, please just let me tell my side of the story."

As Jason contemplated his next move, he lowered his head and placed his hands on his hips. If he let her speak, he knew he would get lost in her eyes and forgive her. If he walked away, he would leave behind a kind, wonderful, fun, charismatic, sexy woman; someone he knew would be irreplaceable. *Although, it could be fun to watch her grovel. If I touch her, though, It's all over. If I hold her, I'll never let her go. Then what? I'm so screwed.*

His indecisiveness told Pam that he cared deeply for her and the situation was hard for him to navigate. She held her breath waiting for him to figure out his next move.

After a long pause, he nodded and turned to face her,

"Okay, you're right. You do deserve to at least have your say."

"Can we sit on the deck? It's such a beautiful day."

He followed her out the door and sat in one of the chairs, keeping his distance.

Oblivious to Pam's movements, Jason focused on the cats as she reached for the bottle of whiskey and cobbler. A layer of aluminum foil had been removed from a white plate, displaying the dessert and two forks.

"What?" Jason raised his eyebrows. "Where did that come from?"

"I need to tell you what really happened. I hope you'll share a drink and desert with me." A smile warmed Pam's apologetic eyes and she poured them both a drink. After he accepted a cup from her, she took a nice big swig from her own cup. She shook her head from the harshness of the alcohol and released a tense breath. Once her nerves had been soaked in whiskey, she began.

Pam described the sequence of events in detail. From the time she and her friends entered the bar and ordered their first drinks, she touched on every important moment of the night. They started off with a couple beers and discussed how her friends noticed the paint on her rear.

After that, they danced in the rain to their favorite song, dried off, did a couple more shots, and rode the mechanical bull. The entire time, she had been thinking about Jason. They talked about the current men in their lives—including, as Grace had so eloquently nicknamed him "Paint-on-your-ass guy".

"When Franklin, or Douglas, whatever his name is, approached me, I made it clear that I wasn't interested. He came on to me; my head and heart were already with you. I blew him off and he grabbed me. I was a little bit concerned, but in such a crowded place, I figured getting on the dance floor would keep him away." Angst spread across Pam's face as she brought back the memory of what happened next. She shook her head and frowned into her drink.

Jason prompted her to continue. "It's okay, Pam. Please go on."

She lifted her eyes to his and found comfort and compassion. She knew at that moment that he spoke the truth; it *was* okay. "I didn't know that the tool followed us until he grabbed my hips and pressed himself into my backside. I couldn't move. He practically hissed in my ear about how women don't deny him. That's when I started to worry. He was doing this in a crowd. I told him not to touch me and tried to shake him off.

"That's when your sister came into the scene and started screaming. At first, I thought she was yelling at him and I was relieved that he would finally let me go. I relaxed a little and squirmed one more time. He released me a split second before her fist landed on my face. Everyone stopped what they were doing." Unable to disguise her pride, Pam ended the story with, "I defended myself. Plain and simple."

After she finished, Jason pursed his lips and nodded before he gulped a shot of whiskey. He raised his eyes and lifted one corner of his mouth in a half-smile. He had a feeling that what she stated was exactly what had happened. His sister had a history of telling tall tales. After days of pondering, he'd figured it was time to get to the bottom of the story once and for all.

"I'll admit that your version of the story is completely different than Olivia's. I really do want to believe you, Pam." He needed a moment to think, so he closed his eyes and sighed. "Listen, I have an idea." He pulled his phone out of his pocket and dialed his sister's number. A tap on the speaker icon allowed Pam to hear the entire conversation. When Olivia answered, he placed a finger on his lips indicating to Pam she should remain silent.

"Olivia, I've been thinking about what you said happened at the Rockin' S the other night. I have a couple more questions."

"Why are you so confused? I told you what happened; it's not the same story that the twit from next door tried to sell you." The annoyance in her voice made

Jason raise his eyebrows and glance at Pam.

"Tell me who started the fight. Did Pam touch you first, or did you touch her?"

"Seriously, Jason. Does it really matter? I'm your sister and that bitch hit me. That's all you need to know."

"That's not all I need to know. Did you start this? Did you confront Pam?"

Silence met his demand for an explanation. He let out a heavy sigh and put his elbows on his knees. He ran his hands through his hair and when his sister still didn't answer, said, "God damn it, Liv. You have no idea what you've done. Pam and I had something really special, something that I've never found with any other woman. And you ruined it because you're a selfish liar."

Surprised at her brother's reaction and how calm his voice was, Olivia stuttered, "Well…I…um…Jason. I had no idea that she was anything but a neighbor. Some floozie that you picked up. And I didn't really lie. I may have just stretched the truth. Besides, anyone that wants to mess with my man—"

Jason cut her off and corrected her in a harsh tone, "You mean anyone that your man wants to mess with? You knew he was a womanizer and a player when y'all started dating. How could you even think that he wouldn't have been guilty in this case? How many times has he cheated on you, again?"

"Six. But Jason..."

He tapped the end icon and stared at the phone. After a few moments, his thoughts had been collected. Through pursed lips, he muttered, "Son of a motherless goat."

Pam giggled at the phrase and Jason lifted his head. "I guess I owe you an apology." He reached his hand out toward her and held his breath as she hesitated. "Please take my hand."

After what seemed like a millennial, Pam accepted Jason's hand. They stood and embraced. He tilted his head. A smile tugged at the corner of his mouth. He tucked a loose lock of blonde hair behind her ear, his fingertips brushing her cheek.

The sensation was so gentle, chills ran up the back of Pam's arms.

"Please forgive me. I promise I'll never doubt you, again."

Anticipation got the best of her. She closed her eyes and parted her lips. Waiting a lifetime for his lips to meet hers made her question her action. She frowned and opened her eyes. Jason stood so close she smelled the whiskey on his breath.

"Waiting for something?" he teased, unable to stop his grin from widening.

Pam sneered playfully and pressed her lips to his.

Jason wrapped his arms around her waist and bent

over her, trying to get as close as possible. The heat of her skin radiated through her shirt and he remembered the feeling of his body covering hers. "You're so beautiful," he whispered as his lips traced a line from under her ear to her lips.

The scruff on his chin tickled Pam's neck and she giggled. More than just the kiss had made her swoon. The thought that she may be falling for a simple rancher warmed her heart. They could learn so much from one another. "Can we promise to not let anything like this get between us, again?"

"Mmm hmm." Focused on the placement of his hands and where he wanted to touch her next, Jason would agree to just about anything.

"Jason."

His hands roamed from her lower back down, her back side, and rested on her thighs.

"Jason." Pam chuckled. "I'm serious. I need to tell you something.

Reluctant to stop his progress, he hesitated but paused to please her.

"I wasn't looking for someone, but my heart had a different idea." A warm smile spread across her face. "I haven't felt like this in a really long time and I'm afraid it's making me a little giddy. I feel like I'm in high school again. Like you're my first boyfriend."

"Baby girl…" Jason's eyes twinkled and he kissed her gently before he studied her face. "You have no idea how happy you've just made me." His hands cupped her face and he searched her eyes. "Trust me, that's something. I haven't looked forward to spending time with anyone in a year. You've opened something up inside of me and I love how it makes me feel."

∩∩∩

LIGHT FROM THE MOON shone through Jason's bedroom window. He had been reluctant to untangle his limbs from Pam's, but the sweet-smelling cobbler sat on his dresser just waiting to be devoured. Besides, the appetite they worked up over the past couple hours drove his desire in a different direction.

"Mmm, this is fantastic," heaping another forkful of cobbler into his mouth, Jason closed his eyes. "Just freaking amazing. What is this called again and how did you learn to bake like this?"

"My grandmother's secret recipe for brown sugar peach cobbler. It's been in my family for generations. But I'd rather not discuss my grandmother while laying naked beside you."

Jason laughed and offered a bite to Pam. A piece of the fruit plopped onto her skin making his desire change directions again. "Don't move," he said and set the plate on the nightstand before licking the dessert off his baby girl.

Holly & Bella

Wednesday, August 23, 2017

"HOLLY, BELLA, YOU remember Pam?" Jason reintroduced Pam to the two mares in adjacent stalls. "They like to hang out here in the barn sometimes. I think it's a comfort thing for them. That and this is where I feed them, so every time they see me, they run into their stalls."

The barn smelled of hay mixed with leather; exactly what Pam would expect from a horse barn. "Why are there stall doors on both the outside and inside of the barn?"

"I've heard stories of too many tragedies where barns have caught fire with the horses trapped inside. The outside doors are never closed unless someone is hurt or needs special attention. They are free to come and go as they please." He ran a hand down Bella's neck, "Horses can judge weather better than humans and place themselves in the safest area. If I chose what I thought would be safe for them, I would probably be wrong."

"So interesting!" Pam stared at Jason; his knowledge extremely attractive.

"Hey, hand me a brush from the tool bucket between the stalls, please. Grab one for yourself, too."

Together, they brushed the loose hair and dirt off Bella's back. Jason showed Pam how to flick her wrist to loosen the dirt instead of just pulling the brush over the hair.

"I'm going to put you on this girl. Bella will be more understanding to your needs. She used to be a show horse in 4-H and county fairs. I picked her up when her sixteen-year-old owner started to show interest in other activities besides horses—namely boys."

"Well, hello there, Bella. You're so pretty." Pam rubbed the horse's soft nose with her fingertips. Bella nuzzled Pam's hand in return, making her laugh.

"Here." Jason handed Pam a handful of animal crackers. "She thinks you have a cookie." He placed her hand in his, palm up, and showed her how to feed the horse treats. "Fingers flat, like this."

Holly nickered in the neighboring stall and Jason put his hand, full of cookies, under her muzzle. "Okay, okay, here's some for you." He shook his head. "Spoiled. The big girl here is Holly; she is full of beans, as her first owner used to say. She's a sweet girl and spunky as all get-out."

Once the saddles had been positioned and fastened securely, Jason led the horses out of their stalls, then he assisted Pam on her mount. Thankful that Jason talked her into changing into jeans and boots, Pam threw a leg across Bella's wide back. They started off at a leisurely walk to get comfortable in the saddle. Pam didn't need to steer her horse; Bella followed Holly almost step for step. She had a feeling Jason had coached beginner riders before. He had a knack for making people feel comfortable.

A slight breeze blew Pam's hair away from her face. Soft clouds dotted the azure-colored sky. The purple blooms of the Winecup, white outlines of cow birds, mixed with the scent of fresh air, trees, land, and grass, brought a feeling of peace.

Surrounded by open fields on three sides and a fence on the other, Pam allowed herself to relax. The rhythmic sway of the horse under her felt almost like a song. The past two weeks seemed to have flown by and stood still at the same time. She hardly knew Jason but felt like she had been with him her entire life.

As they followed a trail through the pasture, Jason turned around in his saddle to ensure Pam was comfortable and to gauge her form. Even though she told him she was a beginner, her confidence said different. It had been obvious that the adventurous side of her welcomed the new experience.

Jason slowed Holly to a stop and waited for Pam to bring Bella up beside them. He held his hand out, palm up, as if introducing Pam to the land. "This part of our property is so flat that I once watched my dog run away for two weeks."

A loud laugh escaped Pam as she threw her head back. She became a little off balance and worried that she might disturb the horses. The animals must have been accustomed to loud people riding them, though, because they stood completely still. "Oh my god, that has to be the funniest thing I've ever heard." She continued to chuckle. "What a great visual."

Four bison wandered near as they grazed on the opposite side of the fence. Alarmed at their size, Pam whispered, "Jason?" A strange gurgling noise from the snorting bison made her chuckle. "Oh, that's such a funny sound."

"These guys won't bother you. Not through the fence. They know their boundaries and I walk or ride this path every day. They're used to me; we have an understanding." He winked. "Don't get me wrong, you don't want to try to pet them like a cow; they're still wild."

"You used to strictly raise cattle. What made you add bison to your herd?"

As if he had answered this same question a hundred times, Jason said, "Well, for starters, everyone raises cattle. This day and age, to be competitive, you have to do something different." He steadied Holly as she started to pace. "She's a little impatient," he explained. "Doesn't like to stay in one place too long. Anyway, a family friend in Paradise is a butcher and suggested that people are looking for a healthier option to beef.

"We came up with bison because of the way they are raised—no hormones, no steroids—along with their higher concentration of omega-3 fats, B vitamins, copper, potassium, and zinc. It's been scientifically proven that consuming their meat boosts energy levels, memory, and mood. The rest is history."

"Fascinating."

"Spiritually, they symbolize protection, stability, and courage, along with abundance, strength, and freedom. The more I pondered buying a herd, the more I found myself intrigued."

"Sounds like you have a lot in common."

Jason bowed his head, then raised his eyes to search hers. "Yeah. Maybe." Holly started pacing again and he took the queue. "Ready to move on?"

Pam nodded and Jason nudged his mare into a walk. As they began to ride, again, Jason commented on how she didn't seem like a beginner. "How many times have you ridden?"

"Only once, really. On a vacation in Mexico with an

ex-boyfriend." The memory took her back to the negative experience. "But I wouldn't call it a ride."

Jason held Holly to a slow walk alongside Bella as he waited for Pam's explanation.

"In the town we visited, the stable owners didn't care how hot it was when there were paying tourists. On that day, it was close to one hundred degrees and the tour guide wanted to take us on an hour-long trail ride.

"This would have been the third ride of the day for that specific group of horses and they were already sweating, gasping for air, and coughing. I was apprehensive before the ride and told my ex that we should just go back to the hotel. He talked me into getting on my horse anyway.

"About ten minutes into the ride, I stopped and demanded to return to the stables. I felt so bad for my poor horse that I couldn't force him to continue. Luckily, the other people in our group agreed with me and we turned the horses around."

"Wow, that's pretty bold." Jason grinned, pleasantly surprised.

"I searched for a water source and, in spite of the owner's plea to stop, gave my horse a bath to cool it down. He only spoke Spanish and he told one of the other members of our group that there were more tours and the horses needed to work the rest of the day. Apparently, he was also pretty pissed that he had to refund everyone's money.

"I pulled out a hundred-dollar bill that I had hidden from my ex and handed it to the stable owner. I made him promise to not work the horses for the rest of the weekend. I ended up rinsing off all eight horses at the stables."

"And did he hold true to his promise?" Jason leaned forward, his eyes wide.

"He did. The hotel wasn't far from the stable and I stopped by twice to check on him."

"Good for you. What a great heart you have."

"Thanks." Pam chuckled. "My ex was so embarrassed that he left me there—didn't even give me money for a cab to get back to the hotel."

"What a prick."

"Yeah, well, when we got back to the States, I told him to f-off and never saw him again."

"Beautiful, kind, and smart. Talk about fascinating." Jason winked. "How are you doing with Bella, baby girl?"

"Just fine, cowboy."

"Ready to kick it up a notch?" Jason's smile under his cowboy hat let her know that this was going to be the good part.

"Let's do it."

Jason nudged Holly into a canter and Bella followed suit. Pam let out a short squeal and held onto the saddle horn for security. She squeezed her knees for balance and remembered Jason instructing her to keep her heels down. Holding the reins in one hand, she found she didn't need to use them to instruct her mare.

Although a totally different experience, the ease of motion being on horseback beat the excitement of the iFLY with her friends. It had been a unique way to practically fly and feel free. Maybe the company was part of it; Jason brought an exhilaration to her life that couldn't be matched.

The trail followed a narrow river—more like a creek—alongside the pasture and through a small patch of woods. The couple slowed when they approached a small log cabin beside the lake where the river emptied into a large pond. A fishing pier stretched away from the shore.

Jason helped Pam off her horse and, after cantering for almost half a mile, she was so excited that she wrapped her arms around his neck and hugged him tight. His cowboy hat brushed the top of her hair and his three-day scruff rubbed against her cheek.

Her energy invigorated him; he picked her off her feet and twirled her in a circle. Once she was steady on her feet, he held her close but leaned his head back and touched the edge of her face. "How does your eye feel?"

The contact had been so light that she almost didn't feel it. Longing for more, Pam tilted her head, her cheek fitting securely into Jason's palm. "I don't even feel it anymore." With closed eyes, she reveled in his touch and tried not to hold her breath.

It was hard for Jason to believe the level of happiness he felt with the woman he adored in his arms. Captivated by the sensation of her skin under his hands and the flowery scent of her perfume, he couldn't resist placing a few soft kisses on her neck, then a kiss on the tip of her nose.

Each time they were together, he sensed himself being drawn to her more. He couldn't deny the connection they shared; beyond the physical aspect of their relationship, there was something different about Pam. He had never dated anyone quite like her.

He reached for her hand and led her to a bench. "Tell me, what have you been up to the last couple days?" Jason wondered if she'd stayed home and moped around the house like he had. Other than to do his chores, he didn't go anywhere, not even for his normal trip to the grocery store. He just hadn't felt like doing anything.

"I had quite an exciting day yesterday."

"Really? And just what did you do that was so exciting?"

"I went on a skydive date with my friends, Danica and Grace."

"You went skydiving?"

Pam laughed at the way his eyes widened. "We went to iFLY in Frisco. It's an indoor skydiving experience. We had been planning it for months. It was so much fun, Jason. You should go."

"Oh! I've seen people talk about that place on Facebook. It really does sound fun."

"I can't wait to try the real thing one day. Another item on my bucket list that I intend to check off very soon. Maybe for my thirtieth birthday."

"I've thought about doing something like that too, but that's where it stops—at the thought. That kind of thing is just a little too crazy for me. I mean, seriously, what's the point of jumping out of a perfectly good airplane?"

"You have the best lines." Pam laughed and touched his arm. "What have you been up to?"

"Nothin', just the same ol' stuff." Jason lowered his head and focused on weeds that had grown up under the legs of the bench. "I missed you." At the feel of her hand tightening around his arm, he turned and stared into her eyes. Empathy mixed with passion made him grin. They held each other's gaze as he leaned toward her, hesitating when his lips were almost touching hers. One hand went behind her head to hold her in place while he placed a gentle kiss on her lips.

Pam kept her eyes open so she could watch Jason's

eyes turn dark. She smiled under his kiss, satisfied that she had such an effect on him.

"You're driving me crazy," he breathed. He decided to suppress his hunger for a little longer and released her. "Come here, I want to show you something." He stood and pulled a key out of his pocket.

Pam followed him to the small cabin and waited for him to unlock the door. He cringed at the squeak that he had been meaning to fix and motioned for Pam to enter.

A two-room building with a kitchenette and a pull-out couch seemed like the perfect structure to be situated beside the pond. No television, just a radio for background noise. Jason flipped it on and 90's pop music floated through the air.

"The bathroom is through that door." Jason pointed to the only door in the small building. "If you need it."

"Thanks." Pam smiled and turned a small circle in the middle of the room. "This is really great, Jason." She found his eyes examining her; a blush warmed her cheeks. "You're so lucky to have all these great places to explore. What a wonderful area to just get away from everything."

"As my dad would say, 'Luck has nothing to do with it'. He's a workaholic and made sure that my mother, sister, and I all had everything we needed." Pausing to grab two bottles of Dos Equis from the refrigerator, he opened them and handed one to Pam. "This is where I come to think."

She stepped closer and put one hand on his chest; he wrapped an arm around her waist and held her close.

Unable to ignore the warmth of his skin under her fingertips, her breath caught. "Thank you for sharing this with me." Raising on her toes, she stretched to place a kiss on Jason's lips. "It's just lovely." Pam took a couple sips of the beer and lifted herself to sit on the small countertop.

"So, Jason"—liquid courage helped Pam to be bold—"I'm going on a mini vacation with a few friends next weekend. We have a whitewater rafting trip in the Grand Canyon planned; one girlfriend called this morning and told me that there was an open spot. I would love for you to come with us. Would you be able to get away for a few days?"

Jason's grin stretched into a smile. "I've never seen the Grand Canyon. I've always wanted to, but my dad said it was just a big crack in the ground. Never been much for exploring. He's more of a homebody that just wants to farm and ranch."

Pam smiled as a plan began to form. A trip with Jason into the Grand Canyon could be the beginning of something beautiful.

Grand Canyon

Saturday, August 26, 2017

FOUR COUPLES WAITED at the heliport in Las Vegas to board the helicopter, their luggage stacked between them. Pam squeezed Jason's hand. "You're going to love this, I promise." She then wrapped her arms around his neck. He shot her a look from the corner of his eye and she whispered in his ear, "I can't tell you how sexy it will be to have my man beside me in a helicopter. I've fantasized about this moment." Placing a kiss just under his ear, she added, "I can't wait to be alone with you."

Nothing made Jason happier than to see his love smile and express pure joy, except the way she made him feel when her lips grazed his skin. He held her tight and pushed the sexy thoughts from his mind. "Girl, you're going to get me in trouble."

Pam chuckled and turned to talk with her friends. Each of the couples brought a unique element to the friendship. Jeff and Patti met in high school and were now cattle ranchers just outside of Denver. Roger and Benita had made a leap to leave their comfortable jobs behind to open a now-thriving winery. Adam and Cara started a successful company building metal structures and installing fences.

Even though Jason wasn't completely prepared for what this trip entailed, he had told himself that he should be a good sport and accept whatever adventure should come his way. After all, each of the friends talked about how they were thrilled to experience such a fantastic trip; their excitement had been contagious. Still, he swallowed hard as he boarded the aircraft.

∩∩∩

"DIRECTLY BELOW US, you can see where the rafts are taken out of the water at the end of the tour. We'll be flying upstream; I'll explain some of the history in a few minutes. For now, sit back and enjoy the ride."

While they soared over the canyon, everyone remained silent, the view spoke for itself. Cliffs layered in various shades of red, orange, and brown showed where the Colorado River had carved through the rock over millions of years. The blue river provided a contrast Jason had only assumed possible in paintings. *This has got to be the most beautiful thing I've ever seen. How could my dad downplay something so absolutely incredible?*

Adam broke the silence. "I've seen a bigger crack than that." He paused for effect. When Benita raised her eyebrows, waiting for the punchline, he continued. "In my butt."

Laughter erupted through the headsets; Patti shook her head, and Pam wiped away a stray tear.

The pilot pointed out each area in which the group would camp as he flew above the river. Once they reached the spot they would put the raft in the water, he hovered. "You'll start there." The helicopter touched ground beside the Colorado a handful of minutes later and the group disembarked.

Whitewater rafting guides had been waiting for the group to arrive and greeted each couple with enthusiasm. Everyone stood near and paid close attention to the pre-trip instructions. All their items and gear needed to be re-packed into waterproof backpacks and stored in a container on the raft. It was understood that each guest was expected to help load the boat as they prepared to launch.

Keeping busy with the tasks kept Jason from anticipating any perceived danger. The spectacular views of sharp, tall rocks that stretched thousands of feet into the sky mixed with the warm sunshine on his face made it easy for him to forget what they were about to encounter.

"Are you up for a new experience?" Pam winked at him.

Jason forced a smile, staring at her through wide brown eyes, filled with indecision, and then gaped at the boat bopping in the river. "Okay." He exhaled and nodded.

∩∩∩

AFTER DINNER, they all took a few minutes to examine the sleeping arrangements, relax, and change into bed clothes. Heat from an expertly built campfire warmed the group of friends as they settled into chairs placed near the flames. The scent of steak lingered in the air as the guide introduced a bag of marshmallows, graham crackers, and chocolate bars.

"Oh, yeah!" Pam reached for a metal roasting stick, pushed a marshmallow onto the end of it, handed it to Jason, and made one for herself. "This is the best. You guys, I haven't had this much fun in forever. I have missed y'all so much."

"Does that fun include your little dip in the frigid Colorado River?" Adam asked as he began to toast a marshmallow for Cara.

A nonchalant shrug dismissed any fear that she'd had at the time. The class-four rapids had taken Pam by surprise and bounced her out of the raft. Cold water had shocked her into action and she heard the guide's instructions echo in her head as if he'd spoke directly to her: *Listen for my voice, float feet first, stay calm. You'll be okay.*

Once she had been pulled back into the raft, her laugh echoed off the canyon walls. Her friends gave high-fives and applauded her bravery. Jason practically had to force his heart to begin beating again.

As he gazed at Pam now, happy the terrifying incident was behind them, he shook his head. "Damn, that was probably the scariest thing I had ever seen. Until you started laughing. Then I knew you were okay."

"I was a little worried, myself. As many times as I've been down this river, I've never seen anyone go in," Jeff admitted.

"I can't believe you didn't scream for help," Patti said, still in awe. "How did you possibly stay so cool and collected? You acted like you'd done this before."

"I guess the pure adrenaline pushed me to think about how to react. Besides, you only live once; might as well embrace the fun instead of being afraid. Adventure beat out being scared this time."

"What a great story for the grandkids! Another great story." Benita nudged Roger. "I'm a little jealous that it wasn't me."

"Hey, I can help you create your own great adventure

story if you wanna fall out tomorrow," Roger offered, making Benita laugh.

"Speaking of great adventures, have you told Jason about our ghost-hunting expedition in that abandoned building junior year?" Cara raised her eyebrows. "I swear that place is known to be haunted. Your girl, there, dragged us in without telling us anything, sat a ghost meter thingamajig on the floor, and conjured a spirit."

With a wave of her hand, Pam dismissed the fuss. "Ah, it wasn't haunted. It's all just a lot of mumbo jumbo."

"Not haunted?" Benita jumped into the conversation. "*Ghost Adventures* featured it on one of their episodes. Had the same thing happen to them that happened to us. Same voices, same apparition."

Although he didn't believe in ghosts, Jason had no reason not to believe the story.

Patti then reminisced about how the friends had gone cow-tipping one drunken night. "I swear that farmer told my dad it was us. He could never prove it, but anytime we drove past that field my dad brought up how no one was ever caught."

"Yeah, that was your idea." Pam leaned into Patti, touching her shoulder. "Drag-racing down that dirt road with our lights off was also your idea."

Cara added, "We're so lucky we didn't crash. That curve came out of nowhere."

"So, my yearly question." Patti nodded to Pam, "I'm interested in how your answer has changed from last year." She turned to Jason, "One of our friend rituals is to ask: If you could go anywhere for a week-long vacation—money is not an issue—where would you go?"

Without hesitation, Pam answered, "Iceland, for multiple reasons. One, to see the Northern Lights at Christmas. But, also, because I've never found anyone that has been willing to go with me."

"Iceland," Jason repeated the answer. "I've never even considered a trip to Iceland; I don't know anything about it." He tilted his head, interested in learning more. "Maybe I need to do some research."

"Besides it being one of the most beautiful places on Earth, you can do so many things there. Iceland is the epitome of 'off the beaten path.' But that's a conversation for another day. Too many incredible photos to show you. Once you see, you'll understand, I promise." Turning the subject back to Jason, Pam asked, "What about you? What's your dream vacation?"

After a moment of thought, he said, "Alaska." Pam's expression asked for more details, so he elaborated. "Because I want to see snow and mountains. Like, real snow and real mountains."

Without demeaning Jason's response, Jeff said, "Come to Colorado, you'll see some real snow on some real mountains." He nodded to Adam. "Am I right?" The entire group agreed.

Pam jumped on the Colorado bandwagon, "Not to mention bighorn sheep and elk, bears, moose—all the wildlife you could imagine." With a slight gasp and wide eyes, she added, "Vail. We need to go to Vail. My parents rent a cabin there every year over Thanksgiving. You need to come with me this year."

The guide interrupted, "It's about time for us to hit the hay. I want to remind you of the importance of staying near camp. If you end up wandering too far away from the cabins, you may just find some wildlife that you don't want to be face-to-face with—trust me, it's not pleasant."

The cabin assigned to Jason and Pam sat at the end of the row. When everyone left the campfire for bed, Pam draped a blanket over her arm and took Jason's hand. She put one finger to her lips and led him to a place not far away from camp.

"But…" Jason hesitated.

"Just over here. Come on." Amused, Pam coaxed him to follow her out of earshot. Arms outstretched; Pam invited Jason into an embrace. Once he wrapped her in his arms, the sense of danger morphed into a sense of adventure. He'd never broken so many rules in his life as he had on this one trip alone.

Sweet, short kisses quickly became passionate and

hungry. Both of them breathless, Jason admitted, "I've been waiting all fricking day to do that."

Pam smiled under his continued kisses and reveled in the sensation of being loved. A fallen tree made the perfect bench; Pam laid the blanket over it, sat, and encouraged Jason to sit beside her.

After all the talk of travel fantasies, Jason felt the need to ask more personal questions. "Tell me about your ultimate dream; what have you always fantasized about happening that would make your life one-hundred-percent complete?"

After briefly contemplating, Pam nodded. "Professionally, to have my art featured in Hollywood movies and that my husband understands and accepts my passion for painting." She brushed her hair over her shoulder. "Personally, for my loving, sweet, smart husband to give me a couple rugrats to enhance the meaning of my life. Oh, and they must be perfect angels or there's no deal."

That made Jason laugh and look forward to the future at the same time. He could picture having a family with Pam and making a good life with her. When she asked for his answer in return, he said, "Professionally, my life has pretty much been designed by my dad. I don't see any reason to deter from that." His gaze captured the intimidating landscape and he drew in a breath. "A couple rugrats is also on my list. I want to live well. To experience and enjoy the simple things in life."

Jason hid his concern about being in a relationship with someone so different than him but admitted to himself that he thought it could work. *Couldn't it?*

He turned to Pam and gazed into her eyes. "You have brought so much fun and warmth and laughter to my life that I'm honestly not sure how I survived without it for so long." He cupped her face and placed a gentle kiss on her lips.

"Can I tell you something?" Pam asked.

"Anything."

"We've had our little bump and it brought us closer. I need to tell you that before we met, I told myself that I shouldn't be in a relationship for a really long time. After my breakup, I thought I needed to get through some things even though I wasn't sure what those things were." She shook her head and tried to get back on track.

She found his eyes and held his gaze, "I know now that I was just talking myself out of living. What I'm trying to say is that I've really fallen for you. There's no reason to try to deny it. I know what we have and it's literally amazing. I'm amazed at the way I feel about you." Knowing she could talk forever but wanting to hear Jason's voice, Pam made herself pause. The anticipation of Jason's response almost made her second guess her decision to admit her feelings for him.

After Jason found the right words, he smiled, kissed her lightly, and said, "I was really scared when you went into the water. I think it made me realize that what we have isn't just a passing phase." A wide smile stretched across his face. "I've already fallen for you, baby girl. I can't imagine a life without you in it."

The light brush of his lips on hers was so soft, Pam wondered if she imagined it. Her arms fell naturally over his shoulders; she opened her eyes to find his gaze serious. One arm wrapped around her waist and pulled her to straddle his lap. "I love you, Pam."

She ran her hands through his hair, raised one eyebrow, and kissed him hard. Her initiation of desire surprised him and, not wanting anyone to hear them in the midst of passion, he suppressed a groan.

Breaking the kiss, Pam stared into Jason's eyes and said the words she had denied herself for too long. "I love you, Jason."

Their hunger for each other was overwhelming. Surrounded by nature, the couple allowed their primal need to take over.

What Might Have Been

Sunday, August 27, 2017

"WELL, SON." GEORGE Payne had made an unusual stop by the ranch for Sunday brunch. He removed his cowboy hat and poured a cup of coffee before settling in a chair at the kitchen table.

Jason flipped the eggs, added salt and pepper, and placed them on dishes beside bacon and toast. After lowering himself into a chair, he asked, "What brings you by, Pop?"

George picked up a piece of bacon and asked, "Did you have fun on your little trip?"

From the flat expression to the annoyed tone of his voice, Jason understood this visit was more than just brunch. According to his father, men didn't leave their responsibilities to others; he had a feeling there would be repercussions from his time away. Jason knew exactly where this conversation was headed and he didn't like it.

"Yeah, Dad. It was a really fun time. The Grand Canyon is absolutely breathtaking. It's amazing that one little river created that gigantic crack in the Earth." Before he met Pam, Jason wouldn't have opened up to his dad like this; something had changed inside him for the better.

"To be honest, it was really exciting; Pam has shown me so many new things in such a short amount of time." He paused and smiled. "She's so different from anyone I've ever met."

His dad remained patient. "Mmm hmm."

Jason kept talking, even though he knew his breath would be wasted on specifics and that the question had been rhetorical. He didn't care.

"From Vegas, we took a helicopter tour that showed us where we would be rafting, then it set us down in the middle of the canyon. We camped with three other couples, friends of Pam's, and the guide, who was a fantastic cook, by the way."

George's nonreaction didn't stop Jason from telling him how pleased he was with the trip and how much fun they had.

"We had steaks over the campfire. He even made a cheesecake. Pam's friends are really great. They talked about growing up together in Colorado, which is a totally different experience than in Texas. We can't drive an hour in the summer and go skiing."

With pursed lips, George interrupted. "Well, while you were off having the time of your life, you'll be glad to know that there were no surprises and nothing out of the ordinary while you were absent from your post." One of George's infamous ways to let his children understand he wasn't pleased was to leave them hanging in the middle of a sentence. The "pause" had given both Jason and Olivia anxiety on multiple occasions throughout their young lives. This day had been no different.

"Your bovine, equine, cats, and birds all enjoyed twice daily feedings and stayed safe even though their owner chose to ignore their needs for three days."

When Jason didn't bite, didn't apologize for asking for and accepting help, George changed his approach. "You know how I feel about you gallivantin' all over hell and back when there's work to be done. You have too many responsibilities at home to run all over the country chasing a piece of ass."

Another pause had been intended to drive the point home; it had started to work.

"She's trouble, son. I think you can see that." His raised eyebrow indicated that he was right. Period.

At first, Jason had been offended by the insinuation, but through his dad's harsh tone, he knew in his heart that what he said was true. As much as he wanted to love Pam, they really didn't have much of a chance, did they?

"I think you have some thinkin' to do, son. You need to make some serious life decisions. Do you continue to live a life of responsibility that you have been groomed for? Before you were even born, you've been first in line to take over the family farm. "

I've done everything in my power to make this ranch successful so you could simply take the reins and run this place. All you need to do is manage the business, upkeep the animals and land, and this place will continue to provide a damned good life for you and your future family.

"I know you're enamored with this girl. She's gorgeous, she's fun, she's different, adventurous. But that lifestyle isn't you. It just isn't. You aren't the kind of guy who just picks up and leaves and forgets about everything back home so you can go see a crack in the ground a thousand miles away.

"I don't know what you're thinking and I don't know what you're planning with this girl, but you need to remember who you are and where you came from. You're grounded here. Your home is here. It always has been and it always will be.

You may think you're in love, but you can't always believe something that you haven't seen with your own eyes. Son let me tell you, they're all pretty much the same."

"I'm curious, Dad. How am I ever supposed to find out if that's true, if there is someone different than all the rest, if I never experience life? If I never get out of Loving?"

"There's no reason to backtalk me, Jason." George ran a hand down his face. "If your mother, God rest her soul, could see what you're doing now, she would be up in arms. Are you seriously willing to throw away all the hard work that I've put into this farm for the past forty years for some escapade?"

At the mention of his mother, Jason pushed away from the table. He refused to give his dad the satisfaction of knowing that he was still able to push the right buttons. Even though his reaction did just that. *Where does he get off saying such things to me?*

Not wanting to admit that his father was right, but knowing that he had rarely, if ever, been wrong, the harsh—but possibly true—words began to resonate. If Jason were honest with himself, he had been thinking the same thing while they were cruising down the Colorado River.

∩∩∩

THE SOUND of crickets and birds chirping floated

through the air over the pond. Jason refused to spread his negative energy to the horses, so he drove the side-by-side through the trails and trees, to his go-to location for all reasons to escape, good and bad.

The cabin provided serenity and silence when he needed to think. In the spring and fall, when the weather was cool, Jason would break out the fishing poles. The crappie and bass had been easier to catch then. On hot summer days, there wasn't much of a point so he would just sit and think.

The last time he had been there, Pam had joined him for a horseback ride; they'd gotten to know each other better over a couple of refreshing beers and a few passionate kisses. Their conversation flowed from previous experiences together to memories of fun, disappointment, and drama of both of their past lives.

The trip to the Grand Canyon solidified his feelings for her and he realized he had fallen in love. When he said the words out loud during their lovemaking, she said it back. They both meant it; it was real.

Before they fell asleep in the small cabin beside the river, he looked into her eyes and saw a future with her. They would make beautiful babies, raise them to be strong, confident people, and grow old together all the while loving one another completely and unconditionally.

As he sat on the bench at the end of the pier, he

picked apart their time together and found himself wondering what it would be like to be so free. His dad's words made sense.

He's right. I need to be responsible and stay grounded. There's no room for a woman like Pam in my life. Adventure is exciting, sure, but it's not realistic to think that we could just get up and go when we have so much responsibility. There is no in-between; there is either the ranch or adventure.

The more he thought about his dad's words, the more he talked himself into believing what he said. "Do you really think this could work? She's just going to leave you anyway. Remember Jackie? Y'all weren't on the same page and look what happened there. She left you for a rodeo star. Pam will leave, too. Do you really want to put yourself through all that again?

"She's not the kind of girl to settle down and let her family come first. Does she even want kids? What happens when y'all have kids and Pam's off on one of her crazy adventures and dies because of some stupid decision? Huh? Then what? You need to really think this through. In my opinion, you need to call it quits now before it goes any further."

Jason had to think about his livelihood, his business, his family traditions, and what it would mean if he gave all that up for a girl. Once you give it up, you can't get it back.

He decided it would be best to go directly to Pam and let her know this had all been a big mistake. That he can't live this way and even though his feelings are so very strong for her, it just can't be. It can't happen. It's not going to work.

∩∩∩

"LOOK, PAM. It's not you, it's me." The words fell out of Jason's mouth as if someone else spoke. "I'm just a rancher that lives next door. I just don't see how it's going to work. We're two people that are so completely different. How would we ever agree on how to raise our kids?"

"We would raise our kids to be strong confident people, just like we talked about at the Grand Canyon." Baffled at Jason's assumption, she added, "They will learn to be responsible and have fun with their lives; live a life combining each of our best qualities." She shook her head in disbelief. "This is bullshit, Jason. We just had this conversation. Where is this coming from? What's going on?"

"Every time you do something crazy, or each story I hear about the foolish decisions you made with an extremely lucky outcome, I imagine how one of our kids would do the same thing and how I could possibly react like a rational dad."

"Jason." Pam struggled to keep her voice steady. "Do you seriously think that my past decisions—that haven't all been bad, by the way—could possible affect how we raise our children?"

Dust covered the toe of his boot and his focus hovered there while he decided how honest he wanted to be. "I do." He lifted his gaze to study her expression. "Just about every day. That's why this can't work—we're just too different."

Pam did her best to hide how much his words hurt, but the tears fell anyway. "Tell me something?" She sniffled but didn't wait for him to respond. "Did you ever truly care for me?"

Despite the knot in his stomach, he nodded.

"Then how can you just walk away from what we have? You told me that you love me and that you can't imagine a life without me in it. I'm so confused." She stood and began to pace. "How can you say that to me one day and, literally, the next day tell me how wrong we are for each other?

"I feel like we're completely right together. You're kind and funny, honest and passionate. You're not afraid to be yourself and can be a little goofy. It's cute. Who cares that we're so different? Maybe that's why this could work. You know, opposites attract and all." She held her breath, waiting for his response.

Courage took over Jason's emotions and he felt the need to completely express how much he cared for Pam. "Don't you know that I love you? Don't you know that I only feel as free as a bird when I'm with you? I've never been so open to try new things and so excited to show someone that I care about the things that bring me joy. And trust me, I think you would be the perfect person to raise my kids."

If she only knew how much it pained him to say these words, she may have empathized.

"I don't want to lose someone that I care so much about. I know it sounds crazy but if I leave now and you kill yourself doing one of these crazy excursions, I won't feel so bad.

"If we were to get married and have kids, start a family, and you die…" He paused and lowered his head. "I don't know that I could go on. How am I supposed to raise a family without you? I love you too much and I know I'm being selfish. I would never ask you to not be you. But this just isn't me."

Some women would have accepted defeat in this moment and moved on, but not Pam. She tried to tell him that it could work, but he wouldn't listen. With tears running down her cheeks, she said, "I love you, Jason.

That's all that matters. I love you."

As if they would never see each other again, Jason pulled her into a tight embrace and they held on for a moment too long. He almost gave in to the pleading from his heart and kissed her; he wanted nothing more than to feel her lips on his. Just one more time.

Instead, he pushed away reluctantly as his dad's words repeated in his head. *She's just going to leave you anyway. One way or another.*

"Let's just think about this for a while, let's see what happens." Her stomach queasy and her knees weak, she begged for more time.

"I'm sorry Pam. There's nothing left to think about; it can't work." He turned and walked out her door, leaving her emotionless, breathless, speechless, and standing alone on her porch steps.

ᕫᕫᕫ

BLUE PAINT FADED to shades of grey as Pam's absentminded brushstrokes covered the canvas. White highlights acted as rays of sun struggling to break through a stormy sky. Unable to concentrate, she allowed emotion to flow unobstructed from her fingertips. When she had done this in the past, she had been shocked to discover the finished product.

Multiple layers of tears had dried on Pam's cheeks

over the past few hours. Each time she tried to tell herself it was for the best and that she's not really in love with Jason, another round of sobs escaped her throat. She even went as far as telling herself that it was stupid to cry over something that never was.

The song "What Might Have Been" came on the radio, Pam's vision blurred yet again. Lyrics about not knowing how things could have turned out hit home. She didn't want to let it go, to turn and walk away or just say goodbye, as the song suggested. *Why is this so damned hard?*

She remembered the day they met. She watched him come out of the chicken coop, moving his feet in a full-on river dance. She almost smiled.

She remembered wrangling emus with him.

She remembered the first time they made love and she began to cry again.

Heartbroken, Pam finished what started out as simply blue paint on a canvas. When she focused on the image, she took a step back. Grey storm clouds covered most of the initial blue. A woman with short blonde hair knelt in the foreground reaching out with one arm. A cowboy walked away through a sliver of green pasture toward a barn. A windmill turned with the approaching storm.

Scissors sat on the counter beside the sink and Pam

picked them up without hesitation. Her long blonde locks seemed to unintentionally attract attention. It had been fun to use her best feature in her favor when she had been younger, but things had changed.

One chunk at a time, Pam severed eight inches of her hair so it reached just below her shoulders. Exhausted, she slumped into the chair in the corner of the room and leaned her head back against the wall. She closed her eyes and let her thoughts run rampant. *What is it that I really want? How is my life going to play out? When is the man meant for me going to enter my life?*

She forced herself to breathe, to relax, and opened her mind. She concentrated on her breathing for several minutes before a vision began to take shape. In her premonition, a little boy and a little girl ran through a hay field laughing, singing, and playing Ring around the Rosie. The sun was low in the sky, on the verge of setting. A light breeze blew the little girl's long blonde hair; it was the perfect summer day.

Then Jason came into the picture. He was happy, smiling as he sauntered over to where the little ones played.

The little girl squealed with delight as her daddy picked her up and began to laugh hysterically as he twirled her around. He kissed her hair, sat her on his hip, and reached for the boy's hand. They walked hand in hand, away from Pam's view, toward home. Their home.

Inspired by different emotions, Pam swiped the tears from her cheeks, moved the blue painting aside, and replaced it with a blank canvas.

Anchor Management

Saturday, September 2, 2017

SATURDAY AFTERNOONS had always been a time for relaxing after all the chores had been completed. Jason routinely woke early to feed the cats, horses, and donkeys and harvest eggs from the chickens.

The remainder of the morning had been spent cleaning and filling the water tanks all around the property, as well as counting heads of bison as he rode the fence line to check for needed repairs.

On the way back to the house, Jason spotted his friend, Nick, parked in his driveway, leaning against his Jeep. He pulled the side-by-side next to his old friend and lifted his chin in greeting.

"Hey, Shaggy." Nick rubbed his clean-shaven chin with his fingers; Jason shook his head as he grasped the meaning. "The year-end Labor Day Anchor Management meeting begins in an hour. You ready to go?"

"Ah, man." Jason shook his head. "I'm pretty tired. I think I'll sit this one out." He wasn't about to let on to the real reason he didn't want to spend the day with people but knew Nick would never let him use the 'tired' excuse.

"Dude. Come on. It's Labor Day weekend. You can't possibly think I'm going to buy that you're too tired to make it to your favorite event of the year. Not this year. This is the last hoorah on Lake Graham. Let's go."

Nick was right. Jason had only missed Labor Day on Lake Graham once—last year when Jackie ran away with ol' what's-his-name. If he didn't show, everyone would know something was wrong. Again.

"It's going to be a great day. Everyone is going to be there. Even some new 'everyones'." He paused and waited for Jason to relent. "Burgers, beer, and bikinis. What's not to love?" With raised eyebrows, Nick didn't back down.

"Okay, okay. You twisted my arm." A smile twisted his lips. "I'll bring the usual."

"Great! Oh, and you might want to shave." Nick shrugged. "Just sayin'. See you at Kindley Park in thirty?"

With a smirk, Jason answered, "Make it forty-five."

∩∩∩

SIX PONTOON BOATS, tied together in the middle of

Lake Graham, bobbed with the motion of the waves. A mix of couples and singles laughed, bathed in the sun, and downed beers while reminiscing about past outings. A few new faces had joined the crowd and seemed to fit right in.

Anchored near the sandbar, the drop-off provided an area to jump in for a quick dip while the waist-deep water had been a better place to play.

Even though Jason wasn't completely excited about spending the day surrounded by people—especially if one of those people wasn't Pam—these were his friends and they always found a way to make everything better.

He hadn't told anyone about Pam because he wasn't sure where the relationship was headed. It wasn't his style to bring just any girl around his group of friends; when he was serious about someone, everyone knew.

Country music from The Highway blared out of a portable speaker tied to someone's phone playing XM radio. Lucky for Jason, none of the typical sad songs had been on the set list, yet.

Girls screamed in delight as they sat on their guys' shoulders and played chicken. Splashing and laughing echoed off the water and other friends sang with the radio; the sounds of summer made it difficult for Jason to be sad.

He tried his best not to focus all his attention on Pam, but he hadn't been able to get her off his mind. His head told him that he had made the right decision, but in his heart, he wondered if he had made the worst mistake of his life.

She would fit in perfectly with all these crazy cooters. E*veryone would just love her.* This crowd would get such a kick out of everything she has done in her short life. They love a good adventure, which is why Jason enjoyed spending time with these particular people. They were exactly the opposite of him and he got his kicks by observing their innocent but sometimes risky antics.

So why is Pam any different?

Nick plopped down beside Jason and nodded toward a petite brunette with curves in all the right places. "She might be a little picky, but she's willing to do most anything." Jason felt an elbow nudge his arm. "You should talk to her." Nick winked.

Everything about Miss Texas screamed perfection. Impossibly white teeth framed by a beautiful, obviously practiced, smile. Accentuated by plump, kissable lips, it had been hard not to stare. Large brown eyes, lined with black eyeliner, didn't need fake lashes.

Her bikini had been a little too small over her ample breasts, which, Jason had been positive, was most likely intentional. Most people would use the word gorgeous to describe her; in his mind, Jason did.

Her eyes never left Jason's as she worked her way

through the crowded boat to sit beside him. "I'm Grace," the young lady introduced herself in a high-pitched tone. "I'm twenty-four, a student at UNT, and love animals, the sun, and cowboys. My favorite pastimes include long walks on the beach and parties on pontoons." She held out her hand and Jason shook it.

The moment she began to talk, Jason's mind started to wander; she wasn't his type. Her head bobbed from side to side while she spoke and she had a confidence that seemed forced. She almost sounded like a walking advertisement.

He flashed a polite smile that didn't quite reach his eyes. "Nice to meet you. I'm Jason." She looked familiar, but he couldn't place where they may have met before.

While she explained more about herself, his mind wandered; he'd started to compare her to Pam. After a few minutes, the brunette pursed her lips, stood, and went back to her friends, who were on a different boat.

A couple beers later, Nick made his way back to sit beside Jason. He could tell that something was off but hadn't initially wanted to ruin the day with deep conversation.

When he asked what was wrong, Jason lifted one shoulder. He gazed into nothingness as he continued to nurse his beer.

Nick's muffled voice reached his ears as he spoke to

someone on the opposite end of the boat. "It must be a girl. I've never seen this look on his face before." Having given his friend enough time to think, Nick made the decision to push Jason into talking. "Dude. You got it hot for this girl, don't you?"

Jason had been so focused on his thoughts that he didn't hear his friend until he repeated himself.

"Dude."

Blinking away internal visions of Pam and the way she moved with confidence while wrangling emu's or riding a horse, Jason found Nick's eyes. "Sorry." He looked down at his feet, then at his beer, and back up at his friend. "What?"

"Oh my God. You're in love, aren't you?"

Jason tried to take another drink only to realize that the can was empty.

Nick handed him a cold one from the cooler. "Well?"

Unable to hide the emotion any longer, Jason admitted, "Yeah, I guess I am." He leaned back in his chair, popped the top, and took a long swig.

Nick's smile spread across his face and he let out a loud whoop. "Hey, y'all, listen up." Silence fell over the group as he called attention to himself. "Jason's in love!"

"Oh man. That's not cool, dude." Jason shook his head. For the first time that day, he chuckled and genuinely smiled.

A few of his closest friends wandered to his boat, offered a "cheers" with their drinks, and asked questions in quick succession. "Where is she man?" "Who is she?" "Do we know her?" "Where have you been hiding her?"

Jason raised his hands in surrender. "Okay, okay. One at a time."

These friends had the most genuine affection for one another and were thrilled to hear that their friend had found someone special.

"She's new in town. She's an artist, a painter, and teaches classes in Dallas. We met on accident just before the Williams' wedding. After that, we've only seen each other a few times, but she's great."

He couldn't hide his excitement or the twinkle in his eyes as he continued to describe the woman he loved through a wide smile. "Kind, thoughtful, adventurous, gorgeous. So much more. Y'all just need to meet her— you'll love her, I know it.

Miss Texas finally realized who Jason was talking about. Her best friend had definately found a keeper. Even more serious than before, said, "We must go meet this girl you love. Right now." She looked around the boats bobbing with the waves and held everyone's attention. "Well, what are we waiting for? Let's go."

∩∩∩

HER HAIR CUT SHORTER, too short for her typical ponytail, Pam pushed blonde locks from her eyes and frowned at her impulsive decision. Multiple different colors were spattered across her white tank top and short jean shorts. *I think I have more paint on me than the canvas.*

Horns honked in the distance and Pam tilted her head, as if pointing an ear toward the sound could help her determine the origin. Voices calling her name forced her from the studio.

Who is making such a ruckus?

When Jason spotted her rounding the corner of the house, his heart did a slow roll. Without a doubt, he knew that this was the only girl for him. The one person he longed to be with every second of every day.

Ten people in swimwear stood beside three trucks. Most of them barefoot with wet hair. None of them looked familiar, but they seemed harmless. Confused by the strange scene, she closed the distance, but before she could ask the question on her lips, Jason stepped from behind two of the half-naked people.

Pam stopped in her tracks as he started toward her. An ear-to-ear smile donned her face and tears welled in her eyes. Both hands raised, almost on their own, and covered her mouth. The attempt to hide her emotion failed.

Words alluded her as Jason sauntered her way with open arms. The gesture didn't need explanation. She trotted to him and leaped into his embrace. He lifted her into the air and twirled her in a circle. "I'm sorry, I'm so sorry," he whispered in her hair.

After he put her down, neither of them released their tight hold. One arm wrapped around her waist as the opposite hand reached into her shorter locks and settled on the back of her neck. "You're so beautiful. I love your hair." He stared into her eyes and spoke the words he had been dying to say for the past three days. "I love you, Pam. I love you."

Oblivious to the group of people watching them, Jason tilted Pam's head and claimed her mouth with his. His head swam in the happiness that this woman brought to his life and he vowed to never let her go.

Pam breathed him in as if his aura renewed her life during most gentle but passionate kiss she'd ever experienced. It was that instant that confirmed she would never leave him. She gazed into his eyes, "I love you, Jason."

When he finally released her, he kept one arm around her waist and presented her to his group of friends. "Everyone, this is Pam. The amazing woman I told you about." He nodded to the love of his life, "Pam, this is everyone."

In unison the entire crowd cooed, "Hi, Pam."

Grace waved to her and winked. Pam's eyes widened and she giggled. "Hi, everyone."

Alternate View

THE COUCH IN JASON'S living room sank under his weight. He reached for Pam's hand and invited her to sit beside him. "First, let me say, again, last night was beautiful. You're beautiful. My love for you is so strong, stronger than anything I could even imagine. I meant it when I said you are the only one for me."

Jason's warmth spread from his hand to hers and Pam squeezed it in response. She sat sideways on the couch so she could look directly at him. "I'll never forget the twinkle in your tired eyes when you said you love me for the hundredth time." The slow blink and tilt of her head joined what seemed to be a permanent smile.

"Like I said, my family is coming over today and we need to address them as a couple. You're ready for this, right?"

"Yes."

Jason and Pam spent most of the previous night talking about what life would be like in the future – how things would certainly change for them and what would stay the same. They agreed to be more open to each other's passions and try new things. Both compromised and in the end and realized how little should actually have to change.

Pam confessed that without Jason in her life, she would miss out on a change to become grounded and have a real home for once. Her parents didn't have many friends and because of all the time they spent away from Denver, it had never really become a home.

Jason discussed what it meant to grow up in this house and continue to live here. He hoped to offer his family the same experiences and traditions that his parents had given him. Few of his memories had been negative and Pam envied him for that.

"Jason, we're here!" Olivia called as she and their father entered the homestead.

Nodding to Pam, Jason smiled and responded, "In the living room."

Pam stood as Jason made the introductions. "Dad, this is Pam Waite. Pam, this is my dad, George Payne."

"A pleasure, Mr. Payne," Pam reached for the elder Payne's hand.

He offered a reluctant smile, shook her hand, and

removed his cowboy hat. "Please call me George. The pleasure's all mine, Miss Waite."

"Pam," she insisted.

George nodded. "Pam."

"We've met already." Olivia raised one eyebrow. "But certainly not on the right terms." She offered a smile. "It's nice to meet you, Pam."

"Thank you." Confused, Pam squinted.

"I'm leaving Douglas. I want to thank you for being honest and bringing to light something that I had been denying for far too long. It's over between us."

"He doesn't deserve you," Pam encouraged.

Once they all chose a seat and Jason served freshly brewed sweet tea, he sat beside the love of his life and began the speech he prepared. "I'm glad y'all are here. Pam has been the subject of some of our recent conversations and I thought it was time to include her while we discuss our future.

"Dad, I'm in love with Pam and I hope you will welcome her into our family. With open arms, no questions, no exceptions."

Jason turned to study Pam's face and smiled at her.

"Even though we have such different backgrounds, how we were raised, and how we lived our lives, we share the same morals, values, and agree on what means the most to us.

"The three most important words in the English language – trust, love, and respect form all the most important foundational aspects of both our lives."

The blank expression that George had mastered over the years offered no insight into his thoughts. He leaned back in his chair and took a long drink of sweet tea before he spoke. "Son." He paused and looked at each of the young adults in the room, "I'm proud of you for going after what you want. And I'm proud of you for finally shaving that shaggy face of yours. Finally, you look like a presentable young man."

An audible sigh escaped Jason and he smiled wide at Pam. He knew better than to interrupt, so he remained silent.

"I remember when I realized my true feelings for your mother. It was 1990 and we had a couple of the same business classes at A&M. Even though I had spent most of my youth farming, your granddad encouraged me to go to college so I could learn different aspects of farming that he didn't know.

"Her ultimate dream was to have a degree in equine science; she wanted to breed and train horses. Instead, she changed her major and became a schoolteacher, so she could spend her summers with you kids.

"I digress. After we dated for a couple months, we met each other's families, and her dad didn't think I was good enough for her." Staring through the air, he looked as if he watched a movie in his mind. "She broke up with me and left school early. I was devastated, not that I would admit it to anyone. All my friends thought she was just some girl, but to me, she was everything.

"Well, I attended a party at one of the frat houses just before summer break and she was there with another guy. I couldn't take my eyes off her. She was breathtaking in her big hair, off-the-shoulder midriff shirt, and ripped jeans. I promised myself that I wouldn't let her get away, again, so I interrupted her conversation with said 'other guy' and took her by the hand to the back yard. I professed my love for her and she cried, told me that she never stopped loving me, either. After that day, we were never apart."

George smirked and brought his attention to his children.

"Won over that hard ass SOB that you called grandpa. He just wanted what was best for his daughter; I can relate." The smile he offered his son and Pam conveyed his acceptance.

∩∩∩

"ONE OF MY FRIENDS will be here in a few minutes and I think you might enjoy experiencing what he does for a living." Jason's wry smile intrigued Pam.

"Okay," she dragged out the word as she squinted at him and wondered what he had up his sleeve. "And what might that be?"

"It's a secret. If I tell you, I'll have to kill you."

Pam feigned a surprised look, covered her chest with one hand.

"Trust me, you'll love it."

Reassured by Jason's insistence, Pam wrapped her arms around his neck and kissed him as if they had been together for years. "I love surprises."

A text message interrupted their intimate moment and Jason smiled. "Cover your eyes."

"What? Why?" Pam's eyebrows furrowed.

"Because it's a surprise. Do I need to blindfold you?" *Hmm, that could be fun.* Sexy thoughts about what could happen later that night entered Jason's mind and he forced them to the side. "Come on, let's go."

With one hand in his, and her other hand covering her eyes, he led her toward the barns. He glanced back to find her peeking between her fingers. "No fair. No cheating." He stepped behind her and replaced her hands with his.

"But I can't see." Pam giggled.

"Yeah, that's kind of the point."

They rounded the corner of the horse barn and stopped before he opened the gate. The faint scent of gasoline reached her nose. There had been no sound to join the smell, so Pam couldn't determine what kind of vehicle sat before them.

"I smell fuel. What are we doing?" Pam asked.

"Ready to go for a ride?" Jason whispered in her ear.

She exhaled to calm her nerves. "Yes."

Jason removed his hands to reveal a small plane that had been hidden behind the barn. When the realization of what would take place set in, Pam became so giddy she clapped her hands and jumped up and down. "I love planes! This is going to be awesome." She turned, wrapped her arms around Jason's shoulders, and kissed him, again. "Thank you, Jason. This is great."

"Tuck is a friend that my dad and I have known forever. He gives us rides around the Loving area quite often. Every now and then, he'll stop by and take us to lunch." Jason pointed to the long, flat patch of pasture that had been kept cropped short with a purpose. "Even has his own landing strip." With love in his eyes, he kissed her hair and admitted, "I knew this would be right up your alley."

ᑎᑎᑎ

"THERE," JASON SPOKE into the microphone on his headset and squeezed Pam's hand while he pointed to a group of bison. "That's the west herd. They are forty-five strong and continue to grow. This is the best way to get an accurate count; it's hard to see everyone from the ground."

Pam allowed adrenalin to take over; her smile and wide eyes showed Jason how much she enjoyed herself. Taking it all in, her head turned from right to left "And that? Is that the cabin?"

"It is. That trail leads back to the barn, see it?"

Pam nodded and sent up a silent prayer. *Please God, don't let this end. I want to feel this excitement every day of my life. Please let this be the real deal. Even if Jason doesn't have tricks like this up his sleeve forever, please don't ever let me lose the feeling that I have right now. I know I can love him forever.*

"That's the east herd, and over there is our main hay pasture. We produce enough to feed all our own animals, plus sell some for a profit." Jason's thoughts mirrored Pam's. *Please God, don't ever let her get bored with me. I know my love for her can provide everything she needs. I want a family with this wonderful human being. She will be the best mother, the best friend. She's already been the best thing ever to enter my life.*

Tandem

Saturday, September 16, 2017

DANICA AND GRACE waved at Pam as Jason parked his truck beside their cars. A small airport—not unlike the landing strip on Jason's property—sat on a patch of farmland just outside of town. Locals frequented the small diner in the makeshift hanger.

Pam greeted her friends with a wink. "Hey, y'all. I'm so glad we could meet up for brunch."

"I'm more excited about after brunch." Grace bounced on her feet. "Can we jump first?"

A glare from Pam and an elbow in the ribs from Danica that made Grace yelp didn't go unnoticed. "Jump?" Jason turned to Pam and lifted his eyebrows.

"Yeah, about that…" She gave her best flirty shrug as her voice trailed off.

"Oh, no. No. Not today." He did not share Pam's excitement.

Her words ran together as she expressed her excitement through bright eyes. "This is going to be great; you'll see. I called Tuck and arranged a special day for us all to jump together."

The friends entered the diner and found a table near the window; Tuck waved from a table at the far end of the restaurant.

"We're really going skydiving? All of us?" It had been impossible for Jason to hide his shaky voice.

Twisting her hands, Pam nodded with enthusiasm.

"Well, I guess your bucket list gets one more check after today. Hopefully it's better than the iFLY."

"It already is." Her smile widened and she looked at her friends. "I'm so happy y'all are doing this with us."

∩∩∩

AFTER THEY SUITED up and received an abundance of training, they boarded the plane and buckled up for the ride. Jason remained nervous; he tried to talk the butterflies out of his stomach as they rose to the jumping altitude. Pam, however, could hardly contain her excitement. She observed the odd look on Jason's face and asked if he would be okay.

"Tell me, again why we are going to jump out of a perfectly good airplane?" Straining to be heard over the loud engine, Jason squeezed Pam's hand.

"This is the ultimate test of trust, just one of the things that you have done for me that has convinced me of your true feelings. I can't tell you how much it means that you are showing your vulnerable side."

"I'm not gonna lie. Baby girl, I'm scared shitless. But I know this is what you want to do, so I'm right here by your side. I know how much it means to you and I'm willing to go down whatever road makes you happy."

Tears formed in Pam's eyes; his profession of love gave her all the feels. "Thank you for doing this with me. Even though I love nothing more than to hear you say that you love me, it's acts like this that prove it. I know you would go to the ends of the Earth to make me happy, and I will do my best to do the same for you."

"It's time." Two tandems stood and pointed to Pam and Jason. They went through the motions of hooking up to the men that would control their jump.

"This has to be one of the best jump days we've had all summer. Perfect temperature, perfect sky. Just sit back and enjoy. We'll do all the work."

During the preparations, Tuck indicated that Jason and Pam had recently fallen in love and had asked their jump partners if they could make their jump extra special.

Once they had been literally pushed out of the plane and began to free fall, Jason and Pam found one another in the air. The tandems followed Tuck's instructions and made it possible for the lovebirds to kiss as they fell toward the Earth at over two hundred feet per second.

∩∩∩

WITHOUT KNOCKING, Jason entered the studio to find Pam adding the finishing touches to her latest painting. Country music played in the background and floated swiftly through the air. She swayed her shoulders and hips to "Blue Ain't Your Color," one of her favorite songs, and twirled as she added more paint to her brush.

Two adults stood at one edge of the canvas and walked away from the observer; a little blonde girl in pigtails sat on the man's hip and a little boy walked between the couple, holding both of their hands. The house and barns in the distance at the far end of the hay field resembled Jason's.

The sun had begun to set and red, pink, and orange highlighted the sky. Jason's breath caught in his chest and his heart raced. *That's us. How surreal. Just beautiful.*

Naturally, his arms wrapped around her waist and he stood behind her, watching in amazement as she added paint to the canvas. He kissed her under one ear and whispered, "Hi, baby girl." She leaned into him and added another layer of color that changed the painting slightly enough to add passion to the portrait.

"This is my vision of our future; the beginning of our happily ever after." She turned in his arms and asked, "What do you think?"

Jason had no response. Passion turned his eyes dark and he kissed her deeply. His hands explored her back and ribs, finally resting on her hips.

"So, you like it. I'm glad."

As they danced in the middle of her studio, she leaned her head back to allow him access to her neck so he could trace kisses to her chin.

The short jean shorts she wore enticed Jason to explore her thigh while he dipped her. The tight white tank top and cowboy boots simply added to the allure. He breathed his passion into her as he held her in his arms; he understood the love he had for her would never fade.

EPILOGUE

Christmas, 2017

"I CAN'T BELIEVE YOU booked this trip, Jason." After flying for over twelve hours, the couple stepped off the plane in Reykjavik, Iceland.

They checked in with their tour guide and got on the road beginning a week of adventures. During the first excursion, an Icelandic horseback ride into the Helka volcano, a private guide led the horses along the ridge of the inactive volcano and beside hot spring pools.

Excited to explore as much as possible, they both jumped at the chance to swim in the natural hot springs of Landmannalaugar.

The next tour in a super Jeep took them past waterfalls, through gorgeous landscapes, and had been able to reach areas that tour buses couldn't. Jason enjoyed watching Pam as she appreciated every second of their time in the foreign land.

∩∩∩

WHEN THEY ARRIVED at the Blue Lagoon resort and Spa, Jason led Pam to their suite. In awe that the room provided access to their own private area of the lagoon, she placed her purse on a table and wandered to the floor-to-ceiling glass walls.

"Unbelievable. Just. Wow." Pam turned to Jason with wide eyes. "For once, I'm speechless." She reached for him and, with tears of joy, kissed the man she loved—the one who she had been sure was her destiny.

"Awe, baby girl, don't cry."

"I just love it. I just love you. I'm so happy. I never dreamed I could be this happy. You're everything to me. In my deepest fantasies, I never believed I would find someone who understands me the way you do."

Holding her tight, Jason suggested, "Let's go in the lagoon. You'll be amazed by the cleansing and purifying powers of the sulfuric waters."

"Have you been doing your research?" she teased.

A brochure lodged in his hand and he shook it as an answer. He led her to the patio, helped her out of her clothes and followed her down the stairs into the warm water.

"Can I tell you something?" Sweet kisses traced her

neck as he pulled her close, again.

"Of course," she murmured, enjoying the touch of his lips and fingers on her skin.

"I brought you here because I knew that it was your dream to see the northern lights."

A grin turned Pam's already beautiful face even more radiant. "They're breathtaking, just like the hotel, just like you." She faced her love. "You're so good to me, cowboy."

"There's another reason."

Pam tilted her head and gave him her total attention.

He sat and pulled her onto his lap. "I want you to know that there will never be anyone else that means as much to me as you do. I've never felt the excitement, passion, and joy that you've brought to my life. You make me feel alive, baby girl." After a brief kiss, he continued. "I never want to spend another night without you by my side. Pamela Marie Waite…"

She gasped; her eyes widened and she held her breath. He had never used her full name before. Nervy butterflies fluttered in her stomach. *Is this really happening? Is he going to…*

Jason wore the most confident, sincere, intoxicating smile Pam had ever witnessed.

"Will you do me the pleasure of spending the rest of your life with me? It would make me the happiest man in the world if you would be my wife." A solitaire diamond set on a platinum band appeared in her line of vision.

Pam could hardly contain her joy, "Jason. Oh my god. Yes," She hugged him as tight as she could, then backed away, tears rolled down her cheeks. After she kissed him gently and with as much love as she had in her being, he slipped the ring onto her finger.

"YES, YES, YES!"

Thank you for reading!

Please consider writing a short review wherever you purchased, rented, or borrowed this book. Reviews help readers find their new favorite stories and authors improve their craft.

Also by Kristi Copeland

TEXAS SUMMER NIGHTS

Somewhere Outside of Sunset - Book 1

Home in Paradise - Book 2

OTHER WORKS

Oakdale

COMING SOON

Heaven Scent

Scan the QR Code to be directed to Kristi's author page:

SCAN ME

About the Author

KRISTI COPELAND is the author of contemporary and book club fiction. She lives in Texas with her husband and multiple critters on their ranch. When she's not writing, Kristi enjoys spending time with close friends, wine tasting, and cat collecting.

www.kristicopelandwriter.com

Let's get social :

Kristi Copeland (Instagram)
Kristi Copeland - Writer (Facebook)
Kristi Copeland (Goodreads)